A HOT CHRISTMAS MIRACLE

A Hostile Operations Team Holiday Story

LYNN RAYE HARRIS

The Hostile Operations Team® and Lynn Raye Harris® are trademarks of H.O.T. Publishing, LLC.

Printed in the United States of America

First Printing, 2020

For rights inquires, visit www.LynnRayeHarris.com

A HOT Xmas Miracle
Copyright © 2020 by Lynn Raye Harris
Cover Design Copyright © 2020 Croco Designs

ISBN: 978-1-941002-60-5

Chapter One

December 18TH - HOT HQ

GENERAL JOHN "VIPER" Mendez looked up at the knock on his door. "Come in."

He'd sent his aide home early today so there was no one to announce visitors. The lieutenant had a new girlfriend and he still needed to find the perfect Christmas present, so Mendez had told him to go. It was only a week until Christmas and time was running out for the kid.

Thankfully, he had his own perfect gift tucked away for Kat. A beautiful white gold necklace with four shining diamonds—one for each of them, and one for each of their children. Though Mendez had never met his son, who'd died in a car accident as a child, Roman was always on his mind. He wanted Kat to know it, too.

The office door opened, and his heart flipped in his chest at the sight of the woman standing there— the very pregnant woman with vibrant red hair that grew longer by the day, and glowing cheeks that said she'd been out in the cold just a few minutes ago.

"Kat." He bolted up and hurried to her side. She smiled as he put an arm around her and drew her close. "What are you doing here, *solnishko?* You should be resting at home."

She rolled her eyes. "Johnny, you cannot be that forgetful."

It took him a second. Her coat was buttoned up, but he realized that she had a cocktail dress on beneath it. "Oh, shit."

"That's right, mister. We are invited to President and Mrs. Campbell's private gathering at the White House tonight. Your suit will be here in a minute. Ghost went to fetch it for me."

"You didn't drive yourself, did you?"

"I'm pregnant, not helpless."

He knew better than to push her further, but hell, she was his entire world and the thought of something happening to her out there on slick roads —or any roads—was more than he could bear.

2

He'd already lost her once—and lost the son he'd never known—and he wasn't going to let it happen again.

He closed his eyes as he pulled her close and pressed his lips to her hair. She smelled like sunshine and vanilla and everything that was right in the world. His heart beat for her. For her and the child she carried. He needed them more than she knew.

"I know you aren't helpless," he whispered against her temple. "But I love you and our baby, and I don't want you doing anything alone right now, okay? Wait until the baby comes. Please."

She squeezed him. "Okay, Johnny. But it's not dark yet, and the roads are clear. I knew you wouldn't remember if I didn't come and remind you."

"Phones, Kat. We have them. They are these remarkable little devices that connect people across miles. You can say anything you want and the person on the other end will hear you."

"Smartass," she laughed as she slapped him playfully on the shoulder. "Truthfully, I thought you'd try to weasel out of it if I didn't show up ready to go."

He stepped back to blink down at her. Guilt pricked him at the knowing look on her face.

"Okay, maybe I would have. Not because I don't like President Campbell, but you never know who'll be at these things. I fucking hate politics."

Kat shook her head. "Baby, you need to take a page from Matt Girard's book and start saying *firetruck* every time you want to swear. For the sake of our child's language. You firetrucking hate politics, am I right?"

He couldn't help but chuckle. "Fine, I hate the firetruck out of them. I just want to do my job to the best of my firetrucking ability, not play games with politicians."

Her blue eyes sparkled as she gazed up at him. "Campbell likes you. He owes you nothing less than his life and his presidency, so I wouldn't worry about games tonight."

"I didn't mean him. I mean the others who could be there."

"Johnny. It's a private gathering—only the people he likes. Garrett and Grace will be there. You don't think Campbell would invite his son-in-law to a political meeting, do you?"

Mendez thought about Garrett "Iceman" Spencer for a moment. Ice was as tough as they came. And even though he'd had a mother who taught manners and etiquette for a living and had therefore practiced her skills on him quite a bit, he

4

still had rough edges that he didn't apologize for. No, the president wouldn't very likely invite his Special Operator son-in-law to mingle with political donors or senators whose favor he wanted to court. Because Ice wouldn't pretend to like anyone he didn't have to.

"No, I don't think he would."

"Precisely. Ah, here's your suit," Kat finished as Alex "Ghost" Bishop appeared in the open door, carrying a garment bag.

Ghost strode in and laid the bag over a chair. "I've got everything covered, General," Ghost said. "If you'd like to get out of here."

Mendez looked at his wife and his second-in-command. He was outgunned on this one and he knew it. Kat arched an eyebrow and grinned knowingly. Ghost had a poker face that didn't give a hint to his mood.

Mendez swept the bag into his hand. "Fine. I'm getting dressed. Kat, sit down. Ghost, stop yanking my chain with that general business."

Ghost's grin was sudden. "Sorry, Viper. Can't help it. I'm thrilled as shit you pinned it on. Everyone is."

Mendez didn't have to look down at his uniform to know there was a star on each shoulder. He'd felt the weight of those silver stars every moment since he'd first put them on. "I'm not unhappy about it either. Just not used to it yet. I thought I'd die a full-bird."

Kat snorted delicately. "As I have informed you many times, you do *not* know everything."

He laughed. "No, apparently I don't."

"I will tell you something else you don't know," she said. "I'm starving! So hurry up and change. The baby and I want to pig out at the White House tonight."

"On my way."

"And no sneaking out of the bathroom in that escape tunnel!" she called after him.

Mendez laughed as he shut the door and started to change. If he hadn't bolted from HOT HQ that day back in the spring, using the false door and tunnel in the private bathroom he currently stood in, he wouldn't have found Kat again. And he wouldn't be the happiest man in the world today.

Chapter Two

THE WHITE HOUSE WAS A BEAUTIFUL BUILDING AT any time, but especially so at Christmas. Kat and Johnny were admitted after undergoing a security check and then ushered to the second-floor central hall, which was part of the private quarters the president and his wife occupied. President Preston H. Campbell III was a handsome man with iron gray hair and a booming laugh. He came over to greet them personally. His wife Helena joined him, hugging Kat and asking when she was due.

"The thirty-first," Kat said. "New Year's Eve."

"Oh my," Helena Campbell exclaimed, taking her elbow gently. "I think we'd better get you to a chair."

Kat laughed. "I feel fine. Really."

And she did. It was no picnic having a baby at

nearly forty-four years of age, but she had always been exceptionally fit. She'd exercised regularly during her pregnancy, jogging right up until the doctor had told her not to anymore. Now she walked, doing at least two miles a day on her treadmill.

"You look fabulous, I might add," Helena said. "Still, please humor me. Come and talk to my daughter, Grace. She's due in April—though I suppose you already know that since Garrett works for your husband."

"Yes, ma'am, I do," Kat said as she accompanied Helena over to where Grace sat with one of her sisters—Charity, Kat thought.

"Oh please, call me Helena tonight."

"Yes, ma'am—Helena," Kat finished, laughing.

"Mrs. Mendez," Grace said with a smile as they approached. "I'm so glad you and the general could make it."

Introductions were made—it was indeed Charity sitting with Grace—and then Kat took a seat with the women, accepting a virgin cranberry spritzer from a waiter.

"Your mother has made me call her Helena tonight," she said. "I think you should call me Kat."

Grace smiled. "Okay then. Kat."

It wasn't that the women didn't know each other

or like each other. It was just that Johnny was in charge of the Hostile Operations Team and she was his wife. In the military, the lines of formality were drawn rather strictly—and Garrett Spencer was enlisted, not an officer. It was protocol and tradition to separate the ranks, and Kat wasn't about to insist it be otherwise. Yet tonight she could be Kat instead of Mrs. Mendez or the commander's wife.

"Congratulations to you and your husband on his new rank," Grace said.

Kat followed her gaze to where Johnny stood with the president and a couple of others, so tall and handsome in his suit. The gathering was casual, but nothing was ever truly casual when you were invited to the White House, so Johnny looked resplendent in a dark navy suit with a white shirt open at the throat. No tie for him. He'd refused to wear it. And she was glad because he looked absolutely stunning with that hint of skin showing. President Campbell wasn't wearing a tie either, she'd noticed.

"Thank you," Kat replied. "Nobody deserves it more in my extremely biased opinion."

Grace laughed. "Well, I'm not as biased as you and I'd still agree. I don't think there's any man my husband admires more than yours."

The talk turned to other things then. Due dates,

genders, and potential names for their babies. It was the kind of talk that Kat wouldn't have pictured herself being a part of just a few short months ago. She'd thought her window of opportunity had closed. She'd certainly never considered she would reunite with the man who was the love of her life *and* have his baby again.

Sadness wrapped around her heart at the thought of the son he'd never known. The son taken from them too soon. She put a hand over her belly almost without thought. She loved this little one who would soon make an appearance, but she missed her son. Roman had been a sweet boy. He'd reminded her of his father with his dark good looks, and he'd been wicked smart to boot. He'd be twenty-one now, with his whole life still in front of him. Anger threaded itself between the lines of her sadness, making her want to scream at the unfairness of life.

She didn't know for certain, but she would always believe her son had been killed by her old FSB handler, Dmitri Leonov. Ordered to do it by mafia boss Sergei Turov because Kat would not shoot an innocent girl for him. Sergei had deliberately destroyed his hold over her because he'd thought she would break. She'd broke all right.

She'd broke free, and then she'd spent years thwarting Sergei at every turn.

"Is everything okay, Kat?"

Kat looked up to find Grace staring at her, concern on her pretty face. Kat swallowed down her bitterness. It wasn't good for the baby. "Yes, fine. I'm sorry. My mind wanders sometimes. Pregnancy brain."

Grace laughed. "I'm beginning to realize that's a thing. I didn't believe my mother when she told me, but it sure is."

Kat almost said something about her first pregnancy, then bit her lip and didn't. Too hard to explain. Too emotional to have to.

A few minutes later, Helena announced the food was ready and Kat made her way to the buffet with the other women, intent on piling a plate to the max. Drowning her feelings about her lost son with food was a good start. She was happy, truly, but thinking of her first pregnancy made her sad. She didn't want to be sad, not when she had so much to be thankful for.

A male voice spoke just behind her before she reached the buffet. "Hello, Kat."

Kat nearly jumped out of her skin. Then she lumbered around to wrap Ian Black in a hug. "Ian. It's so nice to see you."

He gave her a quick squeeze and set her away from him. "You've put on some weight, I see."

He said it with a grin, so she didn't smack him. "Yes. I have eaten a basketball apparently."

"You look great. And happy. I'm glad you're happy."

"I am," she said, her heart so full she thought she might burst with it. "How are you? I haven't seen you in at least two months."

He shrugged. "Work keeps me busy."

"Yes, well I suspect I also don't see you because of this rivalry between you and Johnny. He likes you, Ian."

"And I have nothing but the utmost respect and admiration for him. Which is why I'm not calling up his wife for a chat from time to time."

Johnny appeared then, slipping an arm around her and drawing her in to the solid warmth of his body. Her every cell tingled at his touch. Her very soul glowed with warmth and belonging. He chased away the shadows and made her thrill to be alive.

"Hello, Ian. Haven't seen you in a while."

Kat looked up at her husband. "I was just saying as much to him, Johnny."

Johnny's eyes filled with love. "Were you? Ian, you need to stop by more often. Kat misses you."

If Ian was surprised, he didn't show it. But she

knew he must be. She did miss him. He'd helped her more than he knew. Saved her in many ways. If she hadn't worked for him during the long lonely years after she'd lost Roman, she'd have gone mad. He'd given her a purpose when she'd lost everything. He'd also brought her and Johnny together again. She would always love him for that.

"I'll make a point of it then," he said.

"Good. Be sure you do. Whatever makes Kat happy is my priority."

Ian's gaze bounced between them. "Do you think I could get a minute of your time tonight, General?"

Kat groaned. "It's always business, isn't it? Neither of you can help yourselves."

Johnny gave her a squeeze. "Maybe not tonight, Ian. Call me tomorrow. Or come by HOT— assuming you're not pretending not to know us these days. And it's John, not general."

Ian snorted. "Not pretending a thing, John. Sorry, Kat, I can't help myself. But yes, I'll make a point of catching up to you this week. Before Christmas."

"Great," Kat said. "Now that you two have settled that, can we please eat?"

Chapter Three

KAT FELL ASLEEP IN THE CAR. MENDEZ DIDN'T MIND.
Snow had started to fall softly, but the roads weren't
slick with it. Christmas carols played on the radio.
Kat loved them, so Mendez put them on whenever
they drove somewhere.

He didn't mind the music, but it also wasn't
something he'd have listened to on his own. His
mother had loved carols, but they also made her cry
for his sister who'd drowned at age three. Christmas
had never been the same after little Ava died. It was
always a teary affair, never joyous as it should be.

Mendez thought of his own son, lost before he'd
ever known about the boy, and his heart ached for
what might have been. A glance at Kat filled his
heart with love and fierce protectiveness. Kat wasn't

paralyzed by her loss the way his mother had been. The baby she carried would never be ignored because she was busy grieving the child she'd lost. Not the way he'd been.

He'd wanted his mother's love and attention, and he'd had it, but it was never an all-encompassing thing. She'd loved from a distance. After his father died a few years later, when Mendez was still in high school, his mother withdrew even further.

And now dementia had stolen the rest of her so that she didn't know him anymore. He made sure she was taken care of, but he rarely went to see her these days. His presence agitated her, so he didn't go.

He pulled into the garage of the home he and Kat had purchased together just a few short months ago. It was a big house, grander than anything he'd ever expected to buy, but it had a yard and plenty of room for a growing family. Not that Kat was likely to get pregnant again, but they'd discussed adoption in the future. His life, once so regimented, was filled with possibilities these days.

"Kat," he said softly.

Her eyes opened, their blue depths filled with the kind of joy that still managed to stagger him sometimes. After everything she'd been through, she was a happy person. It was one of the things he loved about her. It wasn't that she didn't get sad, but she didn't dwell on her sadness. She always found the positive side of things.

"I'm awake," she replied. "Just warm and full and enjoying the music."

"We're home, *solnishko*. You can keep listening inside. Or we can go to bed if you're tired."

"I want to decorate the tree, Johnny."

He hadn't had a Christmas tree in years, but now there was a fresh fir sitting in the living room waiting for the ornaments that he and Kat had bought recently.

"It's nearly ten. You sure you don't want to do it tomorrow?"

"No, I want to do it now. Tomorrow, you could have a crisis in the world and then we won't get it done until Christmas is over."

He chuckled. "God, I hope there's no crisis tomorrow. All right let's go. You start the hot chocolate and I'll put the hooks on the ornaments."

"Let's put on our pajamas first."

"Right. Good idea."

They went inside and down the hall to their bedroom. It was sparsely decorated, like much of the house, but they were working on it as they had time. Kat wanted just the right furniture, the right curtains and decorations. Whatever she wanted was fine with him, so he let her take her time.

Except for the nursery, which was fully decorated and ready to go. She hadn't wanted to wait on that one at all, especially once they'd found out the gender of their baby. He still got mushy inside when he thought of the little girl growing inside her. The little girl that was nearly here.

The thought terrified him sometimes. He was fifty-one years old, a general in the United States Army, nearing retirement if he wanted it, in charge of the baddest ass group of military Special Operators the world had ever known—and he was terrified of a tiny baby girl coming into his life and making him feel as if he didn't know a damned thing or have any control.

He'd strode into war zones with more confidence than he felt over greeting this little girl.

Kat came over and put her arms around him once he'd shrugged out of his suit jacket and hung it up in their massive walk-in closet.

"You're brooding, Johnny. Is everything okay?"

He squeezed her and kissed the top of her head. "Everything is wonderful. Just thinking about things."

"The kind of things you can tell me about or not?"

He sighed as he laid his cheek against her hair. "It's our daughter. What if I can't protect her? What if I fail and something gets past my watch? What if the evil in the world wins?"

Kat squeezed him hard. Then she tilted her head back and stared up at him with a fierceness he admired. Most people wouldn't know it to look at her, but his wife was not a typical wife. Kat had spent years in the Russian FSB—the equivalent of the old KGB—and she'd worked for both the mafia and Ian Black. He pitied anyone who crossed her.

"You won't fail, Johnny. The evil will *not* win. There is you, and all your people. There's Ian and his people. There are men and women we don't even know who are working hard for all our tomorrows. There will always be evil, but there will always be people like us—like you—who fight it."

"You're right," he said, even if it still worried him. But he couldn't let his fears affect her. Kat had enough to do right now. She had to deliver a baby soon, and he wasn't going to upset her. Or activate her protective instincts because he had no doubt she'd go full-on mama grizzly if she felt threatened. He wasn't going to let any threats perforate the bubble of their happiness.

"I know I am. Now get your sexy ass changed so we can decorate."

He turned to unbutton his shirt and Kat slapped him on the ass. Mendez growled at her, but she only laughed.

"Later, big boy. I think when we have finished the tree, I'm going to want to feel you inside me."

"Kat," he groaned. He'd never known that pregnant women could be so turned on all the time, but Kat was. Since about the second trimester she'd wanted to make love as often as possible. He didn't mind, though they'd had to get creative lately as she'd gotten bigger. She'd been small for much of her pregnancy, but the past month or so had really made a difference as she ballooned out.

"You won't hurt me," she said, accurately reading his expression. "I feel fine."

She picked up her sleep pants and top and sashayed toward the master bath where she hummed a Christmas carol as she started the shower. His dick throbbed as he imagined her stripping off her cocktail dress and slipping beneath the spray.

And then, because he wanted to see her pretty, naked body, he finished undressing and grabbed the Christmas sleep pants she'd bought him before strolling into the bathroom to watch her soap her creamy skin.

Their eyes met and Kat's twinkled. "Come to join me?"

"Do you want me to?"

"Oh yes," she said, her eyes raking him from head to toe. "I can think of nothing better."

Chapter Four

KAT SAT ON THE COUCH AND SIPPED THE HOT COCOA she'd made while Johnny hung the ornaments where she told him. She'd hung several as well, but her back had started to ache and he'd made her sit down.

"There," she said, pointing at a blank spot on the tree. "Put it right there."

He dutifully hung the shiny silver snowflake and reached for another. She let her gaze slide over him —from the formfitting black T-shirt to the baggy plaid sleep pants with the drawstring that hung low on his hips. His muscles bunched and stretched as he reached up high to hang the next snowflake.

"This okay?" he asked before he fastened the ornament in place, his eyes meeting hers over his shoulder.

"Mmm, just like that. Stretch a little higher, sweet cakes. Let me stare at your fine ass for a moment."

He snorted and hung the ornament, then dropped his arm and turned. "You came three times in the shower. You trying to get me to make it a fourth?"

Kat smiled. Her body still tingled with sexual satisfaction. She'd have never thought that sex while this pregnant would be a pleasant thing, but she was wrong. Of course they had to get creative to make it happen, but the orgasms were spectacular.

"Would that be a bad thing?"

"Sex is never a bad thing, Kat."

"I didn't think so. Here, sit with me and drink your cocoa."

He picked up his mug and sat down beside her, lifting an arm so she could snuggle into his side. The tree blinked with lights that switched between multi-colored and white. Johnny reached up and turned off the lamp so that the tree was the only thing providing light in the room.

"I love it," she said, her throat suddenly tight. "I haven't had a tree in years."

He hugged her a little tighter. "Me neither."

She tilted her head up to meet his gaze. She knew about his past with his mother. He'd kept nothing from her, and her heart ached for the child he'd been. A child who'd grown into a man who still didn't do much in terms of celebrating the holiday. "I'm glad we're doing it together."

"So am I. Even if you're a little picky about where the ornaments go."

She laughed. "But look how pretty it is. If you randomly threw ornaments everywhere, it wouldn't be so nice."

"I know."

She laid her cheek against his chest and sipped her drink. "It's been a great few months. I never thought I could be this happy again."

She felt his lips against her hair. "Same for me."

Beyond the tree, snow fell outside the window, coming down heavier than it had been earlier. It was nothing like the snows she'd grown up with in Russia, but it was still pretty. Not that she wanted snow like she'd had then. This snow was quite enough.

"I'm happy, but I'm sad too," she confessed softly, staring at the twinkling lights.

"I know, honey."

"I wish you'd gotten to meet him, Johnny. He was a great kid."

His hand slid up and down her arm. She hated talking about Roman when they were so happy, but she couldn't help it. And Johnny understood her need, no matter how much it had to hurt him. He'd never made her feel like she couldn't talk about Roman when she needed to.

"I wish I had as well."

Kat sniffled. "I'm not going to cry. We're having a baby and we'll give her all the love we couldn't give Roman."

A sharp pain rolled through her, making her catch her breath. Johnny stiffened as he shifted away so he could see her face. "What's wrong?"

"A contraction."

His face went pale. "Shit, do we need to go——?"

"No. I've been having Braxton-Hicks for days. It's not labor."

He didn't look convinced. "How do you know?"

"Because Braxton-Hicks don't follow a pattern, and they typically don't cause much pain. This one was a little stronger, but unless I start having them regularly, then it's nothing."

"Okay, but you'd better tell me if they get regular."

Kat ran her palm over his cheek. "Relax, General Mendez. It's still nearly two weeks until my due date. I wasn't even dilated at my last check up and Roman was two and a half weeks late. Dr.

Butler says she has every reason to believe I will go full term."

"But what if the baby wants to come early?"

"She could, I guess, but she's not coming right now. I promise you. Now finish your drink and get back to work. I see an empty spot on the tree."

"You're a task master, Mrs. Mendez."

She grinned. "I know. I do it perfectly, or I don't do it at all."

"Got it, babe."

He sipped his drink. It was kind of funny to think that her badass warrior husband was sitting here in his Christmas pajamas, sipping cocoa, and yet he could order a task force into battle at any moment. It was also sexy as hell.

"Kat," he began.

She turned her head to look up at him. "Yes, Johnny?"

"Do you miss it?"

It took her a second. "You mean work? The spy game?"

"Yeah."

She shrugged. "Sometimes. When you're off saving the world and I don't get to be involved anymore, then yes, I do. But I won't put our child in danger, so that's that. No work for me."

She'd been worried about old enemies with

grudges coming after her, but with Dmitri Leonov dead and Sergei Turov in prison, the enemies' list had lost its two most dangerous members. There was no one else with that strong a motive to look for her.

"And you're okay with it?"

She stared at the twinkling lights of the tree. "I have to be, don't I? And I am. I hated leaving Roman while I did Sergei and Dmitri's bidding. If I'd been with him in Novosibirsk, maybe he'd still be alive. Maybe Peter and Ludmilla would too."

Johnny squeezed her shoulders. "Don't think like that, baby. You don't know what would have happened. You might have been killed along with them."

"I know," she said, her throat tight.

"Damn, honey. I shouldn't have asked."

He was frowning hard. She hated seeing that look on his face, so she kissed him. "You love me. Of course you want to know how I feel about being at home while you go to work. We were in the same profession. Mostly," she added since she'd also worked for the Russian mafia. Not willingly, but she had. "You know what it feels like to be involved in operations, the electric charge it gives you sometimes."

"Yeah, but I don't go on missions anymore. My last mission was the one I did with you."

Kat laughed. "That's right. You can't top that mission, so why try?"

He took the cocoa from her and pulled her into his lap. She snuggled up to him, content. "Best damned mission of my life. Even if I wanted to kill you for some of it."

"Ha. You weren't exactly a prince yourself, you know."

"No. When I think of that moment we drew down on each other…" He shivered.

Kat felt that shiver deep inside. She caressed his cheek. She could still see him standing before her with a pistol aimed at her heart. She'd been aiming one at his, too. "You wouldn't have shot me, nor I you."

"I wanted to."

"I know, Johnny. But you didn't."

"I'd throw myself in front of a bullet before I'd hurt you."

She nuzzled his neck. "I already beat you to that one, sexy man." She'd thrown herself in front of Dmitri's bullet to save him back in Moscow. It'd worked. She'd do it a million times over for that result.

"You did, baby. But you'd better not ever do it again."

"I don't want to, Johnny. But I would. For you and for little Elena Katharine." She put a hand over her belly. The baby kicked and she gasped.

Johnny's face instantly changed. "Hospital?"

Kat shook her head, smiling. "No, honey. Tree. Finish adding ornaments for me, would you?"

He kissed her soundly and set her on the couch. "Yes, ma'am," he said, saluting her smartly before picking up an ornament. "Where does this go, ma'am?"

Kat rolled her eyes at him, then laughed. "Right there, General. That big, bare spot that'd bite you in the face if it were a snake."

Men. They often didn't see what was right in front of them. But that's what wives were for....

Chapter Five

KAT DIDN'T HAVE the baby during the night. Mendez worried about leaving her the next morning, but he had to go into work for a few hours. He kissed her at the door and went into the garage to climb into his big black Ram truck.

The snow had stopped during the night and the roads were mostly clear, though more snow was expected later today. In the few years that HOT had been in the DC metro area, it had snowed over Christmas exactly twice. This year could be the third time, though Mendez desperately wished it wouldn't with Kat so heavily pregnant. He had nightmares about being delayed by weather when she most needed to get to the hospital.

Mendez pushed those thoughts from his mind and turned them toward what would happen when they brought the baby home. Matt "Richie Rich" Girard, Alpha Squad's team leader, had told him to get ready for sleepless nights and poopy diapers and spit up. Alex "Camel" Kamarov, a sniper on the SEAL Team who was the oldest of six siblings and therefore claimed to have lots of experience, had waved his hand in dismissal and said babies were a piece of cake. Mendez rather doubted that, but hopefully the truth was somewhere between those extremes.

Ghost was already at work when Mendez arrived. They had a short meeting about current missions and potential hot spots and then Mendez went to his office. His phone rang almost the minute he sat down.

"Mendez," he said.

"Hello, General," Ian Black said. "You got a few minutes for me today?"

"I can spare some time. When do you want to stop by?"

"How's fifteen minutes from now?"

Mendez lifted his eyebrows. "That'll work. Do I

need to ready a team for a mission somewhere, or is this a social call?"

"No team. I'll tell you more when I get there."

"See you soon then."

Fifteen minutes later, Mendez's phone rang again. Lieutenant Connor was on the other end. "Sir, Mr. Black is here to see you."

"Send him in, Lieutenant."

"Yes, sir."

A second later, the door opened and Ian strode in. He was carrying a legal envelope. Mendez stood and went around the desk to shake his hand.

"Ian. What brings you by so early? I assume this is what you wanted to talk about last night."

Ian nodded. "It is." He didn't move to open the envelope, however.

Mendez nodded toward it. "Do you want to show me the papers?"

"I do. But John—you need to prepare yourself for this."

Mendez frowned. "I've been a Special Operator pretty much my entire adult life. I don't think there's much of anything that's going to shock me now."

Ian undid the clasp on the envelope and pulled out some papers. He didn't hand them over, though.

"This might. Look, I don't know how to say this other than to just put it out there. I debated with myself for a while, wondering if the information was good enough—but if it was me, I'd want to see it."

Mendez's gut was turning to ice. "What now? Is someone sending General Comstock to arrest me again? Because I didn't get that vibe from the president last night. Pretty sure he wouldn't have wanted me there if I was in trouble."

Ian shook his head. "No, it's not that." He turned the papers and held them out—and Mendez saw that the top paper was a photo. A photo of a young man who looked strikingly familiar somehow.

"That's... not me. But it could almost be, couldn't it? I've never been in the Russian navy, though I suppose someone could have photoshopped—"

The reality hit him then and the words died in his throat. He knew what Ian was showing him. *Who* Ian was showing him. The young man in the Russian navy uniform *could* be his son.

Was Roman still alive? Or was this a trick of Dmitri Leonov's from beyond the grave? Leonov had been particularly sadistic. He'd been an enemy of Kat's—and Mendez's by extension—for years. Before that, he'd been Kat's handler when she'd been part of the Russian FSB. There was also mafia boss Sergei Turov, who was currently in prison but still potentially dangerous. Sergei had tried to kill Mendez and Kat in Moscow just a few months ago. And Kat believed it was Sergei who'd ordered Roman's death, though it had been made to look like an accident.

Mendez's knees went a little weak and he sagged against his desk, thankful it was there to hold him up.

"His name is Kazimir Rybakov, not Roman Rostov," Ian said. "But they could have changed his name. They wouldn't have wanted Kat to find him."

Mendez's heart hammered. He forced himself to breathe deeply and slow it down. "You don't know for certain it's him."

"No. But the resemblance is notable, wouldn't you say? Not that we don't all have a doppelgänger somewhere, which is why I hesitated. Kat would know, surely."

Mendez thought of his very pregnant wife and his stomach twisted. He had to be logical about this. Resemblances happened sometimes. Uncanny ones, even. Didn't mean anything. But what if…? "I can't show her. Not yet. I don't want her upset when she's about to give birth."

Not only upset but planning how she was going to get a face-to-face meeting with this boy.

"No, you can't show her yet." Ian nodded at the papers in Mendez's hand. "I've given you everything I've found on him. It's not a lot, but he's twenty-one, he was orphaned at age twelve and put into state custody, and he joined the navy two years ago. He is currently stationed in Vladivostok."

Twenty-one. Orphaned at age twelve. It fit, but that didn't mean the young man was Mendez's son.

"How did you find him?"

"How do I find anyone?" Ian asked with a shrug. "I work connections and take my time. But I have to confess this one was an accident. One of my operatives had a meeting with a Russian counterpart—and Kazimir was there. My operative thought the resemblance notable, so he let me know about it. Kazimir is officially in navy intelligence, but he's probably also involved with the FSB."

Anger and hope flooded Mendez in equal measures. Was this boy his son? Or was it just a coincidence. People could share similar features. How many times did you see a picture of someone who resembled a celebrity?

"What the hell am I supposed to do about this?" Mendez growled, more to himself than anything.

Ian looked grim. "I'm sorry, John. That's why I

34

debated telling you. I don't know what you can do. It's a tricky situation."

Mendez held up the papers. "I can start here. I don't have any assets in Vladivostok. And I couldn't send them after him even if I did. My rules are different."

Ian nodded. "Yes, they are. You're a military officer and your organization is funded by the taxpayers. You can't use them for personal reasons. But I'm a mercenary. I can do whatever the hell I want."

"I envy you that sometimes."

"You could always go into private contracting. Retire, hand HOT over to Ghost, and join me over at BDI. Or start your own firm."

Mendez shook his head. "Don't think I'd enjoy that, Ian. HOT is what I need and what I'm good at. I'll leave the private contracting to you."

"Your choice."

He frowned. "I can't go after this kid—but you can. I want to hire you. Get Kazimir Rybakov to DC if you can. If not, I'll go to him. I need to meet him."

"I'll do my best."

"Your best is usually pretty damned good."

Ian grinned. "I aim to please."

Chapter Six

Kat had more Braxton-Hicks throughout the day, but they weren't regular so she didn't worry. She'd been through this before, even if it was over twenty years ago. She called Evie Girard and talked to her for a while, then started working on dinner. Johnny called to say he'd be home early, so she peeled potatoes and carrots and sang along with the carols on the radio. Then she put the vegetables in with the roast she'd seasoned, covered the pan, and slipped everything into the oven.

Three hours later, the house smelled divine and Johnny came striding through the door, looking handsome and fierce in his military camouflage. She smiled at the stars on his shoulders. One star for brigadier general. Her general.

"Baby, what did you cook?" he asked as he set

down his briefcase and came over to wrap her in a hug.

"Roast beef with potatoes and carrots. And onions. I've made gravy as well."

"You shouldn't work so hard at this stage of pregnancy."

She smacked his arm lightly. "Stop it. I should do whatever I want to do."

"I worry about you."

"Don't worry. I'm fine. This isn't my first pregnancy and I'm not fragile."

She met his gaze. Something flickered in those eyes. Something that was bothering him. But before she could ask, he lowered his head and kissed her. By the time he stopped kissing her, she couldn't form a coherent thought in her head.

He led her to the big island in the kitchen, seated her on one of the comfy barstools they had there, and got to work putting dinner on the plates. There was French bread and butter too. He set those out, poured drinks—water for them both—and joined her at the bar.

"Any more contractions today?" he asked.

"A few," she admitted as she buttered a slice of bread.

He frowned.

"They aren't regular. It's not time yet."

"But you have your bag packed and ready, right?"

Kat rolled her eyes. "Johnny. You know I do. You've asked me every day for the past two weeks if I was ready. And I am."

"It's a habit. Sorry."

"You're used to running a huge organization and you like to make sure the details are correct. I get it. But you don't have to manage me. I'm a grown woman who survived for years on my own. I'm fine. If I'd never been through this before, I'd be jumpier about it, but everything is normal. Promise."

He looked troubled again. But he dropped his gaze before she could study him. "You're right. But I love you and I can't live without you ever again—so I worry more than I should."

Kat settled her hand over his. He clasped her hand and lifted it to his lips, pressing a kiss on the back of it. She reached over and palmed his cheek with her other hand. "I love you too, Johnny. I can't live without you either, so I'm planning to do everything I can to make sure you're happy and comfortable. If I think I'm in labor, I'll tell you. So stop worrying, okay?"

He breathed a sigh. "I'll try. It's not in my nature not to obsess over details though."

"I know." She picked up her fork again. "Now tell me about your day. What kind of interesting things happened at HOT?"

Was he frowning? Maybe so. She knew there were things he couldn't always tell her, so she didn't push.

"Not a lot. The world is quieter than I expected right now. Thank God."

"But there is something you can't tell me." His gaze snapped to hers. She smiled. "I understand, Johnny. I'm not a part of the organization. You aren't allowed to share all you know. Don't you think I understand that better than anyone?"

She'd been an FSB agent for heaven's sake. She understood keeping secrets. She understood duty to country as well, though this was her country now. She'd been betrayed by her own and she wasn't looking back. She was as American as apple pie now.

"I know you do. There is something. And I want to tell you, but I can't yet. I will when I can."

She couldn't help the prickle of unease that flared inside. "You're not in danger, are you?"

He laughed, and relief washed through her. "No, I'm not."

Kat stabbed a potato. "That's all that matters to me. That my family is safe—you, our baby, and me. I can deal with anything so long as I have that."

"I know, honey. You don't have to worry. You just work on bringing Elena into the world. I'll do the rest."

Kat lifted an eyebrow. "For *now*. I'm not the kind of woman who intends to sit still for long."

Johnny snorted. "Don't I know it. Now tell me what you want to do tonight. Watch a Christmas movie? Do some more decorating?"

"How about both?"

"Both it is then."

They finished dinner and Kat sat at the island while Johnny cleaned everything up. He put the leftovers in the fridge, did dishes—washing and drying and putting away—and cleaned the stove. Kat sipped the cranberry mocktail he'd made for her and enjoyed the sight of her big bad husband doing chores. It was sexy, and she found herself squirming on her seat as she imagined him doing it in the buff. There was nothing sexier than Johnny Mendez naked. Unless it was Johnny Mendez naked and sliding his cock deep inside her body.

"Kat?"

She looked up to find him frowning at her, but in an amused way. "Yes, my dear?"

"Dare I ask what you're thinking about?"

She grinned. "What do you think it is?"

He leaned against the counter, dish towel in his hand—so hot—and lifted an eyebrow. "I'm thinking it has something to do with sex."

"What makes you think that, Johnny?"

"Oh, I don't know. Could be the glazed look in your eyes, the way you keep squirming on the chair, or maybe it's the way you keep biting your bottom lip as you stare at me."

"Nailed it in one," she said happily. "Think you might want to nail me?"

He dropped the towel and came around the island. He put his hands on the granite, trapping her between his arms. She inhaled the scent of him —soap and steel, gun oil and determination—and shuddered with delight.

"I always want to nail you, baby."

His mouth settled over hers and Kat was lost.

Chapter Seven

DECEMBER 20TH

HE HATED keeping secrets from Kat, but this was the kind of secret he couldn't tell a woman about to give birth. Not when it might amount to nothing. Mendez sat at his desk at work and stared at the photos of Kazimir Rybakov. The resemblance was strong, and yet he wondered if it was real. It could simply be the camera angle, or even a deliberate attempt with Photoshop to make this kid look more like Mendez than he really did.

But that didn't explain Ian's operative, who'd thought the resemblance enough to mention it, did it?

Mendez shook his head to clear the chaotic

thoughts. He remembered Kat last night, how passionate she'd been, and then how happy when they'd settled in to watch a Christmas movie together. She'd laughed at Ralphie's antics as he schemed for a BB gun, and then they'd watched a movie with Kurt Russell as a cool Santa Claus who sang the blues. She'd wondered aloud whether or not he could pull off long hair and a beard like Kurt, and he'd had to remind her it wasn't in military regs.

"Too bad," she'd said with a little pout. "You'd be so handsome, Johnny."

"I already thought I was handsome enough for you."

She'd laughed, and he'd loved the way the sound stroked his senses. He was so gone for this woman. "You are always the best-looking man in the world to me. But a girl can have a little fantasy, right?"

"You have Santa Claus fantasies?" he'd teased.

She'd swatted him and pointed at the television. "Only if he looks like that."

His cell phone rang. He picked it up, glancing at the screen. "Ian," he said after he'd swiped to take the call.

"John," Ian replied. "How're things at HOT HQ today?"

"Quiet," Mendez said. "Thankfully. Got anything for me?"

"Not enough, unfortunately. Rybakov has gone to ground. We don't know where he is at the moment."

Mendez hated the way his heart twisted at the news. He didn't even know if this kid was really Roman, and already he was feeling the desperate pull of a parent wanting news about his child. "Where was he the last time your people saw him?"

"His apartment in Vladivostok. He went in two nights ago and that's the last we've seen of him."

"He knew he was being watched."

"That's what I think too. But I don't think it was my people. They're careful. He wouldn't have known they were there."

"Are you suggesting he's being watched by someone else?"

"If he's really Roman Rostov, then it's possible. Dmitri Leonov might not have been the only person who knew of Roman's real parentage. You gotta admit he'd be a helluva lever to use against you, John."

Mendez's gut tightened. "That's assuming a lot, don't you think? They can't know how I'd react to finding out he was alive. I never knew him. Maybe I wouldn't care."

Ian snorted. "You've married his mother and she's pregnant with another child. You'd care. Any spy worth their salt knows it, too."

Fuck. He hated it when Ian was right—but Ian was right.

"What if the whole thing is a setup? What if Kazimir Rybakov is really who he claims to be and someone with a grudge or an agenda is using him as bait for me and Kat?"

"It's possible," Ian said slowly. "It could also be bait for Kat alone, you know."

Mendez's blood ran cold. Sergei Turov's son Misha was still out there, still capable of carrying out an act of revenge for his father. Sergei was a monster. He'd held Kat prisoner for years with his hold over Roman, and he'd abused her both mentally and sexually. He was in prison now, awaiting execution, but so far he'd managed to avoid the death sentence with delays and bribes.

It would be like Sergei to want to torture Kat one last time. And Mendez through her. Through Misha, he could've organized the whole thing.

"You've heard of Calypso, right?" Ian asked.

"The assassin? She's not someone we've dealt with, but yeah, I know about her. You've had some run-ins with her, I believe."

"A couple," Ian said. "She's an interesting character. She reminds me of Kat in a way. But I digress. The point is she's a master of disguise. She can be tall or short, fat or thin—whatever the situation requires. She made us think she was someone else. So much so that we captured the wrong person because she'd done everything necessary to point us in that direction. Which brings me to my main point—that it's possible to mimic just about anyone if you're skilled enough."

"And yet you brought this situation to my attention when you showed me the photos."

"I told you I had to think about it, but in the end I did what I would have wanted done for me. I'd want to know. You're a smart man and you've seen a lot. You know what people are capable of, and you also know that things aren't always what they seem. You thought Kat was dead for twenty years, and she wasn't. So yeah, it's possible this kid is really your son. It's also possible it's a setup. If it *is* a setup, then he'll turn up whether or not I look for him. So do I keep my people on it, or do I sit back and let it happen if that's what's going on?"

Mendez knew what Ian was asking him. Whether or not he wanted to pursue Kazimir Rybakov. Backing off would give them an answer eventually, but Mendez didn't think he could do that. He needed to know. "Have your people been inside his apartment since he disappeared?"

"Yes. Only six hours ago. He's not there, and there are no signs of a struggle. He left again under his own power, probably in disguise. We're going over surveillance footage from the past two days to see if we can't pinpoint which person is most likely him."

"Keep looking, Ian. If it's a setup, then I'll deal with it when I find out that's what it is."

"And if it's too late by then?"

The knot in his gut tightened. "It won't be. I won't let that happen. Neither will you. If nothing else, you care about Kat. You won't let him get to her if this whole thing goes wrong."

"If this is Sergei Turov's idea of revenge, I'd prefer Rybakov not get to either one of you. Kat would never forgive me if anything happened to you, so don't do something stupid."

Mendez laughed. "I never do anything stupid, Ian. I'm deliberate and methodical. You know that."

"I'm not so sure. You walked into the center of a lion's den this past spring when you were being hunted instead of lying low until the danger passed. That was kind of stupid, don't you think?"

"Not really. I cleared my name, stopped an

assassination plot, and found the love of my life after twenty years absence. I'd say it was the boldest, bravest thing I ever did."

Ian snorted. "Fine, bring that up why don't you?"

"Let me know as soon as you hear anything."

"Roger that. Later, *generalissimo.*"

"Later, 007."

Ian laughed and Mendez ended the call. Damn, who'd have ever thought he'd actually end up liking Ian Black after that first encounter with Ian's operation in Qu'rim?

Chapter Eight

December 23rd

KAT STEPPED BACK to admire her decorations. The house smelled like freshly baked cookies and looked like Christmas had exploded everywhere. There were signs proclaiming things like *Have a holly jolly Christmas* and *Let it snow,* and miniatures trees and ornaments on shelves and counters. There were pinecones, pillows, trays, blankets, reindeer statues, and candles. Everything was frosty and glittering and perfect.

Kat smiled to herself, happy with the results. Maybe she'd gone overboard, but she liked it. She'd never decorated like this before. It was kind of addicting. The HOT ladies would be arriving soon for the cookie exchange—Kat's first ever—and she was looking forward to it. Johnny had frowned last night when she'd reminded him about her little party today.

"Don't overdo it, Kat," he'd said.

She'd rolled her eyes. "I keep telling you I'm not helpless, Johnny. I'll be fine."

And she was fine. She was full of energy lately, and she had a strong urge to nest. She knew it was because the baby was coming soon. This pregnancy was so different from the last. With Roman, she'd been alone. She'd been scared about having a baby, worried about the future, and heartsick that Johnny was gone from her life for good. She hadn't known what to expect, either with childbirth or what her life would hold. She certainly hadn't known that the FSB would control her life so thoroughly or force her to give over the day-to-day care of her son. She'd been young, or maybe she would have fought back harder. On the other hand, fighting back would have only cost her. They might have taken her son from her at birth and never let her see him at all.

Kat put a protective hand over her belly as tears pricked her eyes. She would not allow anyone to take Elena from her. Not ever. She was older, wiser, and deadlier. She'd kill anyone who tried.

"Stop it," she whispered fiercely as she wiped her eyes, furious that she was weepy. Damn hormone overload. "Your life is so good right now. Don't borrow trouble."

Johnny had asked her if she missed operations, and the truth was that she did. She'd been an operator for so long that a full stop had been difficult. And yet she looked forward to being a mom again, to actually raising her child this time, and to sharing the task with her husband. If she wanted to go back to work later, she could. Not exactly doing what she had been doing—too dangerous—but she still had very useful skills that someone like Ian or Johnny could use.

Well, when the time was right, maybe. And maybe it would never be right. Maybe she'd be happy being a wife and mother, things she'd never had a chance to really be before. Both jobs were important. There was also the idea she'd always had in the back of her mind about writing a book. She loved to read, and she'd lived the kind of life that meant she had a never-ending supply of high-octane thriller ideas. Wouldn't that be something? Her, a published author. And why not?

It was half an hour before the doorbell rang. Kat smoothed her hair as she checked her reflection on the way to the door. She'd put on a dark green tunic with black leggings, black half boots, and she'd swept her hair into a loose ponytail. She'd applied red lipstick and dark mascara, and her eyes were bright as she looked at herself approvingly. She looked like a suburban housewife instead of the spy she used to be. She didn't even have a weapon strapped anywhere on her body. Yet another thing it had taken time to get accustomed to.

Instrumental Christmas music played softly as she opened the door to greet her guests. Evie Girard and Georgie McKnight were standing there together. Grace Spencer was getting out of her car along with Brooke Sullivan. Other cars were pulling into the drive, and Kat stepped back to let her guests inside. The house had been quiet, except for Christmas music, and now it was filled with laughter and ladies' voices as the women came in and gathered around the kitchen island, shedding coats and setting down their containers of home-made cookies. Kat pointed them toward the drinks and snacks while she took their coats.

Some of the ladies were at work, but those who could make it trickled in over the next few minutes. Emily Gordon and her sister Victoria Brandon, Sophie Daniels, Christina Marchand, Miranda McCormick, Eva Ryan, Annabelle Davidson, Ella McQuaid, Bailey Jones, Bliss Bennett, and Quinn

Garrison stood around talking with plates of appetizers and drinks ranging from cranberry cocktails —and non-alcoholic mocktails—to sparkling water, wine, and juice.

Kat fixed her own plate of nibbles and joined the ladies in the living room where she'd put out extra seats. They had left one of the overstuffed chairs for her instead of a harder dining room chair and she sank onto it gratefully.

"How are you feeling?" Evie asked.

Kat sighed as she picked up a sausage ball. "Fat."

Grace laughed. "I'm with you on that one, Mrs. Mendez," she said, reverting to her usual mode of address.

Kat smiled. "Please, all of you, call me Kat. Military protocol is for military situations. You are in my home, and I consider you all friends. We have a unique position as wives or fiancées to HOT operators. We're a sisterhood."

Kat eyed Victoria for a second. She'd known Victoria when they both worked for Ian, but only a little bit. She knew that Victoria worked as a contractor to HOT on occasion, though she had no idea in what capacity. Though if Johnny wasn't using the woman's sniper skills then he wasn't being very bright. Kat also didn't know if the other women knew what Victoria did, so she didn't mention that Victoria was more than an operator's wife. That was Victoria's secret to share or not share.

Victoria met her gaze and quirked an eyebrow as if acknowledging that their similarities went beyond marriage to HOT men.

"To the sisterhood," Miranda McCormick said, raising her glass. Everyone echoed her as glasses were raised. They all drank, and then it was back to talking and laughing and eating food together.

"How's the general handling things now that it's close to the due date?" Emily asked.

Kat snorted. "He thinks I'm fragile and unable to lift a finger, naturally. He also fears I will go into labor and have this baby in a matter of minutes rather than hours. He believes every contraction means it's time to race to the hospital. In fact, I think he'd prefer if I checked in right now and stayed until Elena is born."

The women who'd had children laughed and shared stories about their husbands acting much the same. The others chimed in from time to time with stories of friends who'd given birth and swore there was no way they were letting their husbands act like that when they were pregnant. Kat, Evie, Emily, and Grace shook their heads and said, "You just wait."

A couple of hours later, the party was coming to a close when the door from the garage opened and Johnny walked in. Kat blinked and glanced at the clock in the kitchen. "Excuse me a moment," she said to the ladies who were standing and holding coats as they prepared to put them on and walk outside to their cars.

"Is everything okay, Johnny?" Kat asked as she approached him. He was standing in the kitchen, staring at the island, frowning. He looked up as if he hadn't heard her approach, which was crazy because the kitchen and great room were open concept and he could see everything.

"What? Yes, of course." He drew her close and buried his nose in her hair before kissing the top of her head. "You smell delicious."

"It's the Christmas cookies," she said, her body already starting to tingle with awareness.

"Of course. I should say hello to your guests, then I'll go to my office until you're finished."

"We are finished. They're in the process of leaving."

Johnny took her hand and walked into the great room with her. The conversation died as they approached. She knew these women were married or engaged to HOT operators of their own, but her Johnny couldn't help drawing admiring looks from them. He was the very definition of a silver fox.

"Ladies," he said, turning on the innate charm he had in spades. "It's good to see you all. Thanks for coming to Kat's party."

"Thank you, General," they murmured.

"It was delightful," Evie said. Others echoed her.

Johnny gave Kat a squeeze and let her go. "If you'll excuse me, I have some work to do. Don't let me interrupt."

"Grab some cookies on your way," Kat said to him.

"I will."

With polite goodbyes, he left them. Fifteen minutes later, everyone was gone and Kat went looking for her husband. She found him in his office, as he'd said, sitting at the big desk she'd picked out for him and staring at his computer. He looked up, his gaze seeming faraway for a moment. The cookies he'd taken sat untouched on the desk.

"Are you okay, Johnny?"

"I'm fine, baby. Just some shit going on in the world. Nothing to worry about."

"I wouldn't worry except that it appears you are."

"I'm not worried. Really. It's just a puzzle, that's all."

Kat went over to him and he pushed his chair back. She climbed onto his lap and he leaned them backward, his arms going around her big belly as hers went around his neck.

"I love you," she said.

"I love you, too."

"I know you can't tell me everything. I understand it, and I know it's what I signed up for when I married you. In Russia, we were equals. Here, you're the big boss and I'm not even involved in operations. But I know what it's like, and I know when you're troubled. So don't hide how you feel from me, okay? I want to know."

He kissed her neck and her skin sizzled. "Okay. And you're always my equal, Kat. If you weren't pregnant, if I wasn't afraid of losing you again, I'd want you working for HOT. I'd want your mind and your skills on my team."

"Thank you, honey. I appreciate you saying that. But I'm going to be a wife and mommy for a while. Maybe one day I can consult."

"And charge an exorbitant fee for your expertise, no doubt."

She didn't miss the grin in his voice, and she

laughed. "That's right, mister. I will charge what I'm worth."

Johnny gazed up into her eyes. "There's not enough money in the world if we're talking about your worth."

She shook her head slowly, grinning. "Flatterer. Are you trying to get me out of these clothes?"

"I'm serious, baby. You're worth more than money to me. More than anything in this world. I'd do anything for you. You know that, don't you?"

He looked earnest and she slid her palm along his jaw. "I know, Johnny. But there's nothing you need to do except love me and our little girl. That's all I want."

"You already have that. As long as I live."

Chapter Nine

IT WAS SNOWING when Mendez woke up at six a.m. He could see it coming down through the top of the transom window, though he didn't know how much had fallen yet. Beside him, Kat lay on her side, sleeping peacefully. Or as peacefully as possible considering how pregnant she was. She often woke during the night to pee, or because the baby was kicking her, and she was usually exhausted in the mornings.

He slipped out of bed carefully, then went into the bathroom and brushed his teeth before padding back into the bedroom and slipping on the buffalo plaid sleep pants Kat had gotten for him. They were flannel and he didn't usually sleep in them because they were so warm. He preferred sleeping in his underwear though truth be told he'd rather sleep in the buff—except that old habits from his operator days meant he wore briefs, so he didn't get ambushed with his dick hanging out.

He dragged on a grey t-shirt and left the room on silent feet. He went into the kitchen to start the coffee—decaf these days because it's what Kat could drink—and then stood and peered out the window at the backyard. Everything was covered in white, and the snow was fat and thick as it fell. He frowned as he took his phone out and found the weather app.

They could get up to twenty-four inches in the next few days, though that was a long shot. Still, Mendez's gut tightened. Kat wasn't due for another week, but the closer the date got, the more he worried. But he had a four-wheel drive truck and enough emergency medical training to understand the fundamentals of delivering a baby. Not a task he wanted, especially when the baby was his own and the woman was his life. No way in hell did he want that responsibility.

But if he had too, he could.

He placed a call to HQ on his secure line to check on things there. He wasn't scheduled to go in today, but he would if something went terribly awry. Ghost answered and they discussed the situation for a few minutes, then Mendez hung up and went to pour his coffee. He was just taking his first sip when a text from Ian landed.

Ian: *Think we've located him.*

Mendez's heart thumped once, and then he locked it down and typed back. *Where is he?*

Ian: *Novosibirsk.*

Mendez let out a breath. Novosibirsk. Where Roman had last lived with the couple who'd been raising him for Kat. Where he'd been when Kat got the news he'd died in a car wreck. Where he was buried. Mendez remembered standing beside his grave with Kat, not aware at that moment who she really was or that Roman was his. He'd ached for her pain, but he hadn't known it was his pain too. Not until later.

And then someone had started shooting at them and they'd had to run. They'd holed up with Yuri Budayev, otherwise known as the Tiger. That was where Mendez learned the truth about Kat. Yuri didn't trust a soul and he'd ran her fingerprints without her knowledge. Mendez had nearly exploded with twenty years' worth of loss and anger, but they'd worked it out in the end. Thank God.

Still, what was Kazimir Rybakov doing in Novosibirsk?

Mendez: *Anywhere in particular?*

Ian: *He's staying in an apartment near the city center. Not far from where Peter and Ludmilla Yelchin lived before they died.*

The couple who'd been raising Roman while Kat did Sergei Turov's bidding.

Mendez: *Either someone is going to a lot of trouble to set us up or he's searching for something.*

Ian: *The truth maybe?*

Mendez didn't dare hope, and yet he did anyway.

Mendez: *But why now? Why not at any point in the past several years?*

Ian: *He's twenty-one, he's in the navy, and those who had a vested interest in controlling him are either dead or in prison. With the exception of Misha Turov, who likely has more important things to worry about just now. Maybe Kazimir's finally learned something that has him on the hunt.*

Jesus, he hoped Ian was right. It *was* possible. If the kid was really Roman, if he'd inherited even a tenth of the skill his mother had, or even his father, then maybe he'd bided his time until now. Maybe he was on the move because the time was right for him to do so. But what did he know? Would *could* he know?

Mendez: *What's your next move?*

Ian: *Watch and wait. Unless you prefer we kidnap him? Might be a little hard getting him out of Russia, but I like a challenge.*

Mendez: *Tempting, but I'd rather not create an international incident just yet.*

He'd wanted Ian to arrange something so he could meet with Rybakov, not abduct him.

Ian: *Your call, but I like creating incidents.*

Mendez laughed. Then he typed, *Yeah, I know.*

Ian: *How's Kat?*

Mendez looked toward the hallway. It was dark and he couldn't hear anything coming from the master bedroom.

Mendez: *Ready to have this baby. She doesn't sleep well.*

There was a lump in his throat as he pressed send.

Ian: *It's going to be fine. Though neither of you are gonna sleep much after the baby comes, you know.*

Mendez: *So everyone says.*

Ian: *Gotta get back to work, mon general. I'll let you know if anything changes.*

Mendez: *Thanks, Ian. I owe you.*

Ian: *I know.* <winky emoji>

Mendez erased the conversation with Ian, just in case, and set the phone on the counter. He kept things from Kat all the time, because they were mission specific and he had to, but this one felt different. It was personal and it involved her. He wanted to tell her, but all she could do was worry if he did. Strike that—she'd do more than worry. Kat would act, and that wasn't something he needed to deal with when she was about to have a baby. Nothing stopped Kat. Though she was about to give birth, she wasn't your average pregnant woman. Kat was highly skilled and deadly. If she got the idea she had to do something, she would. And Mendez didn't want her doing that right now. They didn't have Kazimir in front of them and they didn't know if or when they would. Mendez wasn't telling her a thing when it could all be a sick joke pulled by their enemies.

Fuck. He shoved a hand through his hair. Part of him wanted to call Ian back and tell him to go and capture the kid, bring him to DC so Mendez could see him in person. So they could take a cheek swab and solve the issue of his DNA once and for all. If he was Roman, then Mendez would go from there. If he wasn't, then Mendez would put the fear of God in him about messing with him or Kat and drop his ass on the Kremlin doorstep. Misha Turov would get the message loud and clear if he was trying to run a revenge plot for his father.

But patience was best, so he planned to be patient. Ian knew enough people that he could arrange for Kazimir to be sent to the States on an assignment. Or maybe somewhere in Europe where Mendez would meet him and learn the truth. There was time. No need to rush.

Mendez finished his coffee while watching the snow come down. It was pretty, and it reminded him of his first winter in Moscow, though there'd been a lot more snow. He didn't want that kind of snow here, not when Kat was pregnant. He turned on the Christmas tree lights because he knew Kat would like that when she woke up. He also put Christmas music on in the great room, turned down low, so she'd have that too. Then he went to the mudroom and slipped on boots, his coat, gloves, and a hat, before going into the garage to get the shovel so he could clear the driveway.

The air was cold, and the snow was steady. He waved at a neighbor shoveling his own drive and then got busy making sure the way was clear if he needed to get Kat to the hospital. His mind was on Kazimir/Roman and how Kat would react if the truth was a miracle. Was it really possible that Roman had survived? Or was the whole thing a cruel setup? It was the kind of cruelty that Dmitri Leonov had loved most. Sergei Turov was more of the bullet-through-the-brain type, but Dmitri believed in fucking with minds. Ripping the real Roman away from his mother and making her think he was dead fit Dmitri's personality. If that's what had happened, it made Mendez wish that Dmitri was still alive so he could be the one to kill him this time.

Only he'd do it slowly, not fast with a bullet the way Ian had done.

Chapter Ten

KAT WOKE AFTER A PARTICULARLY SHARP KICK TO her bladder. She lumbered up and went into the bathroom to pee as the baby continued to kick. Johnny wasn't in bed, but she knew he was home. He'd taken the rest of the week off plus he hadn't come in to kiss her and tell her goodbye. He was always quiet if she was still asleep, but she knew when he kissed her forehead. She always knew.

She brushed her teeth and dragged on a fluffy robe over her pajamas, then shuffled off to the kitchen. There was a pot of coffee and a cup sitting ready for her. She put in some cream and poured her coffee, then headed for the great room. Johnny had plugged in the tree and turned on Christmas music. She knew he did it for her. She smiled as she passed through the room and walked to the front of the house where the dining room and his office lay. She could see him in the driveway, shoveling snow in his buffalo plaid sleep pants and boots.

She laughed softly. Other men might want to put on something more manly, like deer hunter camouflage or something, but not her Johnny. He didn't give a crap what anyone thought. He shoveled snow in his Christmas sleep pants with *Let it Snow* written down one leg and didn't flinch.

Kat returned to the kitchen to fix breakfast for them both. She could tell he hadn't had anything yet because there were no pans in the sink, no toaster sitting out, nothing. Plus, he usually waited for her. She whipped up some french toast and eggs, finishing up just as he was coming back inside. She heard him stomping in the garage and then she heard the door open and the sound of a coat being hung on the peg.

When he sauntered into the kitchen in his sleep pants and gray t-shirt, she had to sigh. His muscles flexed and bunched as he walked, and he had a nice pump from all the shoveling. His face was a little red, from cold and exercise, and he smiled when he saw her.

"Morning, baby," he said as he walked over and gave her a kiss on the cheek. He smelled like cold air and pine trees with a hint of coffee.

"Morning," she replied. "I made breakfast."

"I see that. But shouldn't you be resting? You had a rough night."

She moved away to finish putting the food on plates. "I know, but I'm not tired anymore. It's part of being this pregnant, Johnny. Your body has all kinds of energy because you're about to deliver and you're going to need it."

"Okay, honey." He took a seat at the island and she pushed his plate toward him. "Looks delicious."

She fixed her own and joined him. They often ate at the island, because it was big and convenient, but she'd already thought about how they were going to move to the table when their child was bigger just so she'd learn that a family ate meals together and talked to each other. No telephones at the table, unless Johnny had to have one for work. One of the things Kat had never had growing up was a nuclear family that sat at a big table and talked about their day while they ate dinner together. She wanted that for her kid. At least Roman would've had that with Peter and Ludmilla for a while.

Johnny's phone dinged with a text. She didn't miss the way he glanced over at it, like he really wanted to look, but if they weren't calling him then it wasn't an emergency. He palmed the phone and slid it toward his plate but didn't turn it over.

"You can look, Johnny. I understand."

He shook his head. "It'll wait until after breakfast. Baby, the french toast is amazing."

"I'm glad you like it. I was going to save it for Christmas morning, but we're having a breakfast casserole while we open presents instead."

He stopped eating and leaned over to kiss her. "I love you."

She couldn't help the way her body seemed to melt every time he touched her. "And I love you. This is the best Christmas for me in a very long time."

"Me too." He tucked a lock of her hair behind her ear and went back to the french toast.

Kat nibbled her lip as she toyed with her eggs. She had so many things on her mind lately, and she didn't quite know how to deal with them all.

"What's wrong, baby?"

Kat looked up to find him watching her. She loved how tuned in he was to her, how he just knew when something was off. She also hated it because it meant he could easily worry about her when she didn't want to distract him. "Nothing's wrong. I just can't help but be a little scared about all this. Not the birth," she added quickly. "Raising her. I don't know how to raise a kid. I'm not twenty anymore. And I've never had a normal life. What if I screw it all up? What if I screw *her* up?"

Johnny tugged her chair over close to his and put his arms around her. "Honey, it's more likely I'll be the one to screw her up. I mean how's she ever going to date with me hanging around, growling at boys and cleaning weapons when they show up?"

Kat snorted. "Oh boy, you would, wouldn't you?"

"I would and I will. Little will they know you're just as lethal. Unless you want to clean your guns too?"

She couldn't help but laugh. "Sure, I'll clean my guns. We can lay them all out on the dining room table while we do it. Or maybe the coffee table while she watches a show with a boy. What age can we start this?"

"I dunno. You think five is too early?"

He was about to send her into a fit of giggles. "Five? That's a little early. I'm thinking twelve. She'll be entering puberty and getting interested in boys around then, so why not?"

"Okay, so twelve years old, we clean guns when she invites a boy over. You want to put that in the calendar, or do you want me to?"

"I think we'll remember."

He kissed her forehead. "You're going to be great, Kat. We're going to be great together. I mean yeah, I for sure don't know what the hell I'm doing. But you'll keep me on track. We're going to have a great daughter. She's going to have the best we can give her, and she's going to be smart and more capable than either of us can imagine. Hell, we might have a future president on our hands. You never know."

Kat hugged him tight, tears pricking her eyelids. "I'm glad you're so positive. I am too, really—I just get a little overwhelmed at times."

"You can always tell me the truth, babe. When you're overwhelmed, let me help. We're partners and equals, and Elena is my kid as much as she's yours. I'm changing diapers and getting up in the middle of the night and doing my turn with every-thing—except breast feeding, for obvious reasons."

She laughed. "You're a goofball."

"I can be. Not many people know that, so keep it under your hat, okay? Can't have my reputation as a hard ass taking a hit."

He was teasing her now and she loved him for it. He managed to chase away the doubts with his silliness. "It's our secret. But never divorce me because I'll tell everyone. I'll take out billboards on the Beltway."

"Divorce you? Not possible. That word doesn't exist for me. It's you and me and Elena forever."

"Sounds perfect to me."

"Come on, finish your breakfast. I'll do the dishes and we can watch one of those movies on our list."

"Which one?"

"Whichever one you want, baby."

"A Christmas Carol."

"Then that's the one. Eat."

She did.

Chapter Eleven

DECEMBER 25TH

MENDEZ WOKE EARLY AGAIN, shoveled the driveway again, and went inside to find that Kat was still asleep. He took the casserole she'd prepared the night before from the fridge and put it in the oven, following the instructions she'd left on the counter. Thirty minutes later it was done and Kat came shuffling in, red hair piled on her head in a messy bun as she yawned and mumbled, "Merry Christmas, Johnny."

He put a cup of decaf in her hand and kissed the top of her head. "Merry Christmas, Kat."

He led her to the great room and seated her in front of the tree. Then he returned with a chunk of the breakfast casserole on a plate and gave it to her. He went back for one for himself before joining her. They ate a few bites, then put their plates on the coffee table while he handed out the presents for them to open. They hadn't bought a lot for each other simply because they'd been planning for the baby, plus they already had the things they wanted.

But Kat got misty-eyed over the necklace he gave her. "It's beautiful," she said, and he knew she was close to crying.

"Like you," he told her. He stood and fastened it for her, and she stroked it with her hand, lifting it to look at the diamonds.

"One for each of us. That's so sweet, Johnny."

"That's me, honey. Sweet."

He grinned and she sniffled. "Well, you are. For me."

"For you," he acknowledged. He opened his presents from her—a sweater, a fancy remote control for his man cave, a shirt that said *Baby Daddy* on it and made him laugh, and finally a set of heavy silver desk frames that she'd populated with photos. The first was of her and him together at their wedding. The second was of Roman. Mendez thought he was about eight or so in the photo. The third was blank.

"I thought you could put all of us on your desk. We'll get one of Elena soon," Kat said softly.

His throat was uncharacteristically tight. "That would be wonderful."

Kat put her hand on his knee. "If you want to keep it private, your desk here is fine too. You don't have to take the pictures to work."

He looked up, into her eyes that sparkled with tears, and shook his head fiercely. "No, they go to work with me. I want to look at this family of ours every day I'm there. I don't need reminders of what I do this job for, because I carry you all in here." He tapped his chest. "But that doesn't mean I don't want to have a physical reminder too."

"I'm glad you like them."

"I love them."

He thought of a text he'd had from Ian last night. *He went to a cemetery. Stood in front of the grave-stone for the Yelchins.*

Mendez had texted back a thumbs up because he hadn't wanted to make Kat think he was doing anything. Not that she'd have asked, but they'd been enjoying watching a movie together and he hadn't wanted to detract from what they were doing.

He pictured the young man in the photo Ian had shown him putting flowers on the grave where Peter and Ludmilla Yelchin, and Roman Rostov, lay.

Not that Roman Rostov was the name on the stone. It was Yelchin because they'd been raising him and Dmitri Leonov had told Kat it was better to let everyone believe Roman was their son, not hers. It was a lot of trouble for a setup, but also the kind of thing one did when running a con. Especially if you thought you were being watched—extra points for authenticity.

Kat grimaced and his attention immediately sharpened until she was his only focus. "What's wrong, baby?"

"A pain," she said, trying to smile. "That one was sharp."

The hairs on the back of his neck prickled. "Sharp how?"

"Sharp, like a real labor pain instead of a Braxton-Hicks." He shot to his feet, but she put out a hand to stop him. "Johnny, calm down. It might be a real pain, it might not be. We have to wait. What time is it?"

"Two minutes after nine."

"Okay, good. We have to time the pains. If they're regular, then it's labor. If I don't have another one, we'll call this a really severe false contraction and go with that."

"Where's your bag?"

She lifted an eyebrow. "The same place it's been

every time you asked me that over the past month. Inside the closet, sitting on a footstool. Everything I need is there. I'll also need my purse, which is tucked beneath my nightstand."

"You still eating?" he asked, nodding toward the casserole that she hadn't yet finished.

"Yes, of course," she said, reaching for the plate with a shaking hand. He didn't like that her hand shook. She picked it up and took a bite. "Mmm. How did you like it?"

His plate was empty. He'd polished it off while she opened her presents. "It was delicious. You're a fantastic cook."

She snorted. "I read recipes. And I follow them. That's what it is."

"Well you're a damned fine recipe follower."

She pushed the plate away with the casserole a little over half eaten. "I'm not really all that hungry. If you put this away for me, I'll eat it later."

He didn't like that she wasn't eating, but he nodded and took her plate to the kitchen. He put away the big casserole dish and then he covered her plate and set that in the fridge too. He cleaned the dishes, glancing over at her every once in a while. But everything seemed fine and he started to relax a bit.

"Oh shit," she said, and he dropped the towel he'd been holding and hurried to her side.

"Is it labor? Do we need to go?"

Thank fuck he'd kept the driveway shoveled. The snow was falling again, but he didn't doubt his ability to get her to Riverstone. He'd already arranged with Dr. Puckett to take his wife there for her delivery. Kat's age and her history as an operator, plus her status as his wife, meant he got to pull some strings and get her into the private facility for the birth.

"I think it's labor, yes," she said. "But I've only had two pains in thirty minutes. It's not time to go. You have to wait for them to get closer together. Besides, Roman took eighteen hours from onset of labor to birth. We have plenty of time."

He didn't know what that meant for this pregnancy or why it was relevant. Still, she looked calm. He wasn't.

"You don't think having two in thirty minutes is enough?"

Kat laughed. "Johnny, you really didn't pay a bit of attention in that childbirth class, did you?"

"I did," he grumbled. "But I can't think when you're in pain."

"When they're about five minutes apart, we'll go. Okay?"

"Okay." He didn't like that, but she seemed confident. "You're early, Kat. You kept telling me you had a week to go."

"I was supposed to, but babies do what babies want sometimes. Roman was two and a half weeks late." She smiled up at him. "Looks like we might get a Christmas baby after all—or maybe the day after. We'll have to be so careful about her birthday in future, you know?"

Mendez could only shake his head. "What are you talking about?"

"Her birthday. You don't get double the presents or double the attention when your birthday is on or near Christmas. We'll have to make it special for her, so she doesn't feel overshadowed by the holiday."

"We can give our kid double the presents, you know. We have the money."

"Well, yes, I suppose that's true." She frowned. "But we still have to make her day special. She'll want birthday parties and all the things a kid normally gets. It'll be hard on Christmas day. I really hope she comes tomorrow instead. Not that tomorrow will be easier with it being the day after Christmas."

"So we pick a day earlier in the month, or in

January, and hold her parties then. Big parties at Chuck E Cheese with games and shit."

Sounded like a nightmare to him, but whatever. He'd do it for his daughter and his wife.

Kat laughed. "Oh Johnny, you sure are a scream sometimes. You don't want to go to Chuck E Cheese with a bunch of kids. You'd rather be dropped into a war zone with only your bare hands and a cell phone with ten percent battery left."

"That obvious?"

"Yes, baby, that obvious. But it's a good thought. Parties on a different day, I mean. We'll figure it out. She'll be fine."

He liked that he made her laugh, but he didn't know what to do right now. For one of the rare times in his life, he felt helpless. He was a man of action. A man who got things done and didn't wait for others to do it for him. He planned missions, directed a large Top-Secret facility with men and women who were responsible for keeping the world safe from global catastrophe, and he didn't know what to do at this very moment when his wife was about to have a baby. He couldn't command the baby to come. Couldn't command Kat to get in the truck and head for the hospital until she was ready. He couldn't make *anything* happen and it drove him crazy.

"What do we do now, Kat?"

She looked up at him, her expression softening, and he knew he must have sounded like a whiny kid or something.

"We wait. She'll either come or she won't. So let's stop twiddling our thumbs and do what we usually do, okay? You go into your office and check the news and I'll watch a Hallmark movie. If anything changes, I'll let you know."

"Okay," he said, doubtful. "You sure you don't want to watch one of those holiday specials together?"

She smiled. "You've watched a bunch of them with me. Besides, I want to watch a feel-good romance on the Hallmark channel. You didn't like the one you watched with me before."

"With the prince? No, that was silly."

She rolled her eyes. "That's the point, Johnny. They are all silly and sappy and sweet. They make people happy." She picked up his new remote and handed it to him. "Go program this when you're done with the news. That'll keep you busy for a while."

"Fine." He took the remote and bent to kiss her, then reluctantly went to his office for a quick check of the news and a text to Ian. Then he traveled upstairs to his expansive man cave and turned on the projector so he could program the new remote. He was twenty minutes into a program about restoring a classic car when his phone dinged with a text.

Kat: *My water broke. It's time.*

Chapter Twelve

KAT WAS WAITING BY THE DOOR WITH HER PURSE and coat when Johnny came bounding down the stairs. He ran over to her, concern on his face. She put a hand up to stop him.

"Please get my bag from the closet and be calm. I'm fine."

"You said your water broke."

"It's leaking out now, yes." Leaking pretty quickly, but even that wasn't urgent yet. "The contractions are closer together but not quite as close together as they should be. They might send us home, but Dr. Butler told me I should go when the water broke because of my age. So we're going. Be calm, get your clothes on and get my bag, and we'll go find out if she's coming now or if we have to wait a while longer."

She didn't really think anyone would send her home, but she wasn't telling him that just yet. She needed him to be methodical and cool, like always. A sharp pain ripped through her and it was everything she could do not to let him see how strong the contraction was. There was still time to get to the hospital, of course. With Roman, she'd been in labor over eighteen hours. Her labor had progressed much more slowly with him. Though this one seemed to be a bit faster, it would still be hours before she delivered.

Johnny looked fierce as he ran toward the bedroom. He was back in less than three minutes, her bag slung over his shoulder, wearing jeans and boots and looking as calm as a cucumber. She knew he wasn't, but that's what Johnny did—he got things done and he got them done as efficiently as possible.

In truth, she figured he was relieved to have a job now.

He hit the remote start for his truck, and she heard it rev up inside the garage. Then he opened the kitchen door and hit the button to send the garage door up. "Wait," he told her as he went over and put her bag in the back seat. Then he took her hand and led her to the truck.

"We should put something on the seat," she said, eyeing the smooth leather of the passenger seat and not wanting to leak all over it. She'd put a pad in her underwear, but what if it wasn't enough?

"I don't care about that," he said.

"I do."

"Kat, Jesus."

"Johnny. Get a trash bag or something."

He swore as he stalked over to a shelf and grabbed a giant leaf bag. He returned and put it on the seat, then helped her inside. Kat sank into the cushions, then stiffened as another pain hit.

"Slow down a little bit, okay?" she mumbled to Elena as Johnny raced around the truck and jumped inside.

He reversed onto the drive, hit the garage remote, and sped toward the subdivision exit. They were about ten minutes from town, but Johnny drove like they had a lot farther to go. Kat tried to focus on the scenery as it sped by. The trees were dressed in winter white and snow fell onto the road, though it wasn't sticking because the crews had been out to spray the roads.

"It's so pretty," Kat said, looking at the snow that'd been piling up everywhere. "So damn pretty. Reminds me of Moscow."

"Moscow without onion domes," Johnny said. "Or old palaces."

"*Da.* I sometimes miss those. We were so young and in love, weren't we?"

He glanced at her. "Maybe not so young now, but still in love. More now than ever. At least for me."

She swatted him playfully and then bit back a groan. "Me too, jerk."

"The pain's getting worse, huh?"

"A little. Why do you ask?"

"You called me a jerk. Any minute you'll be threatening my balls and accusing me of doing this to you."

"You did do this to me. I'm pregnant because of you, Johnny. Again."

He reached for her hand and squeezed lightly. "I know, baby. If I could go through it for you, I would."

Kat leaned back and moaned. "I know you would. Oh lord, why did I ever think being pregnant again was a good idea?"

"It wasn't planned, remember?"

"I remember. Oh wow." She clutched a hand to her belly and tried not to move.

"Kat?"

"Just drive, Johnny. Get us to the hospital."

Johnny hit the button on his steering wheel to activate the voice command feature and told it to dial Dr. Butler. She answered on the second ring. "General? Is everything all right?"

"Kat's in labor. We're on our way to Riverstone now."

"Oh boy, this little one didn't want to wait, did she? I'm on my way. Meet you there."

Johnny ended the call and Kat dragged in a breath as the pain ebbed a bit. "You didn't have to call her. They would have called from the hospital when we arrived."

"So I sped up the process."

"The baby might not come for hours. She'll have to go home again, then return when the nurses tell her to." Kat said the words more for herself than for him. She wanted to believe them, but deep down she was beginning to doubt what she said. Roman had taken his time, and she'd expected this experience to be much the same. She'd planned everything based on the last time—and it wasn't happening that way. It should be many hours yet, but her pains didn't feel like it was going to be. Five or six hours tops, maybe. She'd really like that damned epidural now, thank you very much.

"It's her job, Kat. She would have to come and check you out anyway."

"I know. But it's Christmas. I hate for her to have to leave her family on such a special day."

Being married to someone whose holidays were often interrupted—and having led that life herself in the past—she knew how disappointing it could be for those who wanted you around.

Johnny reached over and gave her shoulder a soft squeeze. "Honey, she delivers babies. Babies don't adhere to timetables. This won't be her first interrupted holiday, I promise."

"I know." Another pain ripped through her, and fluid gushed out. "Oh shit," she moaned as pain and fear swirled together. Elena wasn't waiting. She wasn't going to be like Roman in the least. She was coming a lot quicker. Too quick. Had Kat really thought five or six hours only moments ago?

"Jesus, Kat. Hang in there."

"I'm hanging. But I think we need to get there soon, Johnny."

His knuckles whitened on the wheel. "We will. I promise."

Chapter Thirteen

Fuck.

He'd promised her they'd get there soon, but what if he was wrong? It was snowing and anything could go wrong. Hadn't he been worried about this for days? Worried something would go wrong and he'd fail somehow.

Except he hadn't failed yet. They were on the way to the hospital. Kat was moaning beside him, her face white with pain. He hated seeing her that way, knowing she hurt because she was giving birth to their child.

Mendez pressed down on the gas just a bit, wanting to get to Riverstone but also aware road conditions weren't the best and he needed to be careful. They were on a two-lane road, but soon he'd reach the highway and zip the rest of the way to Riverstone. They rounded a corner and he had to slam on the brake, cursing as he steered away from the truck that had overturned in the road.

"Oh," Kat moaned. "You're fucking kidding me, right?"

"Firetrucking kidding, right baby?" He was trying to make a joke, but she glared daggers at him. Not that he could see them since he had his eyes on the road and his heart in his throat, but he felt the murderous intent in her gaze. "Sorry, honey. Say what you want."

"I'm sorry too, Johnny, but I'm progressing too fast. The contractions are much stronger than they should be at this stage. *Sonofabitch!*"

"I'll turn around," he muttered, looking for a way to spin the truck without danger of going into the ditch. He hoped she was calling her contractions a son of a bitch and not him, but who knew? He'd been around women in labor, part of the job sometimes, but he'd never been the focus of their rage for making them pregnant in the first place.

He put the truck in reverse and carefully guided them backward until he found a little spot he could make the turn. In the opposite direction he could see headlights blocked by the overturned truck, but there was nothing coming from the direction he'd been traveling just yet. He made the turn and headed back the way they'd come. He'd have to swing by their subdivision and then hook a right onto a different road that would lead to the highway. It wasn't the most direct route, but it wasn't too much farther than the way he'd intended to go. Not what they needed right now, but the only option they had.

"Johnny," Kat gasped. "Elena doesn't want to wait. I think she's coming."

"She can't come yet," he said in the tone of voice he used to order his subordinates around. Not that he expected it to work with his baby girl, but Jesus, he had to try.

Kat snorted despite the pain she had to be in. "She's not listening to you. Hurry, please. I'm trying not to push."

"I'm hurrying." He pressed the gas and they flew down the road. He raced past their subdivision, and then took the turn toward the highway.

"How much farther?"

"Twenty minutes this way."

"I can't wait twenty minutes. I think you need to pull over."

Mendez felt as if she'd punched him in the gut. Fear and denial rolled over him. But then he dug deep and found his control. He had a huge well of it. Precise, deadly, focused control. He would do whatever it took for Kat and Elena.

He aimed the truck at an empty pull-off spot and skidded to a stop. Then he hit the button for voice command as he jumped out of the truck and went around to pick Kat up and put her into the back seat. She moaned as she clung to him. He hated to move her and yet he didn't have much choice. He couldn't maneuver his way to help her in the front seat.

"What's up, General?" Ian Black asked, sounding way cheerier than he ought to.

"I think I'm about to deliver a baby, Ian."

"No shit? What do you need?"

"An ambulance to take us to Riverstone."

"You got it. Where are you?"

Mendez sent his coordinates with a tap to his phone. He could have called Ghost or any of the operators on duty at HOT. He could have called 9-1-1. But calling Ian was like going straight to the front of the line. Ian was his equivalent in the civilian world, plus he knew Kat better than most. Besides, it was better for a civilian to make heads roll to get his way than for a general in the Army to do it.

"Stay on the line. I'm calling for reinforcements."

"Thanks."

Kat's eyes were squeezed shut and she was panting. "You have to get my underwear off. She's coming soon."

"Okay, baby. I've got you. Hang on, honey."

With tender hands, he managed to remove her underwear. Thankfully she'd worn a loose maternity dress.

"Johnny. Oh God, this hurts. I'd hoped for an epidural by the time she came."

Cold air swirled around them and he got inside the truck so he could pull the door closed behind him. He had Kat's bag that contained her clothes and the blanket they were planning to bring Elena home in. He got that out and prepared to wrap the baby up should she come before the ambulance arrived.

"I can see the top of her head," he exclaimed in wonder. She had a headful of dark hair, too. A rush of love and fear filled him in equal measure.

"Oh hell," Kat moaned. "How did this happen? Why is she coming so fast? It wasn't like this the last time. I had so much time to wait."

But any reply he might have made was lost when Kat screamed in pain. He took her hand, didn't flinch as she gripped him tight. He remembered the training they'd gone through together and started coaching her to breathe. He didn't think she would listen at first, but then she did as he said.

Ian didn't speak, but Mendez knew he was still there. He was glad of it, actually.

Mendez kissed her sweaty brow and told her how much he loved her. Then he prayed for a healthy baby and a safe delivery as he did what he had to do to help his wife bring their child into the world. The next few minutes were the longest of his life. And the most revelatory. He thought he and Kat were equals? No, not even close. She was his superior in every way. There wasn't a man alive who could survive this kind of agony.

Kat breathed and pushed and yelled. In the distance, he could hear the scream of sirens getting closer—but Elena was coming and she wasn't waiting. With another hard push, her shoulders slid free.

"One more time, Kat," he said to her. "She's almost here. You've got this, baby. You're incredible."

Kat's face was streaked with tears, but she pushed again and Elena slid from her mother's body. Mendez couldn't breathe. She was bloody and perfect, and his emotions threatened to overwhelm him.

He wrapped the blanket around her body, afraid to touch her with his bare hands. But he had to in order to clean the mucus from her nose and mouth. The rest of her would wait, and he wasn't going to touch the umbilical cord since the ambulance was on the way.

When he'd gotten her sufficiently wrapped, he laid her tenderly against Kat's chest. Kat was crying, her face red with her exertions.

"Congratulations, momma and daddy," Ian said in the background. "Well done, both of you."

"Ian," Kat exclaimed, her voice hoarse. "I forgot you were there."

"I know. You were doing something more important."

Mendez could see red lights flashing in the snow. The screams of the sirens reached a crescendo as the ambulance pulled up beside them and stopped. EMTs rushed from the vehicle. A moment later, the truck door opened, and uniformed technicians appeared.

Mendez could breathe again.

Chapter Fourteen

MENDEZ SLUGGED BACK SOME COFFEE AND RUBBED his forehead absently. They'd been at the hospital for an hour now and he'd stepped out while Dr. Butler checked Kat over. He was still shaking inside from everything that'd happened and replaying it in his head. They'd been supposed to have a normal trip to the hospital where Kat would progress through labor and deliver their daughter several hours later. It hadn't happened that way. He should have known his wife and child wouldn't do anything the way they were supposed to do.

The door opened to the waiting room and Ian Black breezed in, looking as calm and unflappable as always. Hell, Mendez usually looked that way himself. Today was not that day.

"John," Ian said, coming over and shaking his

hand. "Congratulations, man. So thrilled for you both."

"Thank you."

"Helluva ride though, huh?"

"An understatement." He cocked his head. "Why are you here, Ian? You didn't have to come out to express your congratulations personally."

"I wanted to talk to you about Rybakov. You got a minute for that?"

Did he? He felt like the distraction would be good right now. "Yeah, sure."

"He went to see the Tiger."

Mendez was surprised at that news. "He did? Do you know why?"

Ian shook his head. "No idea. But it means something, don't you think?"

Mendez frowned. He was emotionally drained, but that didn't stop the wheels from turning. "Yuri is an old friend, but he's also a businessman. He'll take someone's money if the price is right. His loyalty is very specific but not absolute. He wouldn't put us in any danger, but he *would* accept payment for information about us if someone had enough to make it worth his while."

Ian nodded. "Yeah, but how did Rybakov know to go to him in the first place? Yuri has never worked with the Turovs to my knowledge. Common criminals according to him."

"You said Rybakov is in naval intelligence. It could be as simple as that. Yuri works with the government from time to time. This kid could know who he is through work. Maybe he's on a mission."

"True." But Ian didn't look convinced.

"Do you have something else you aren't telling me?"

Ian shook his head. "No. It just feels like there's more going on here."

"There's a lot going on. We just don't know what it is or why." Mendez forced himself to think. "Was he followed by anyone besides your people?"

"No sign of anyone."

"So he very likely left his apartment in disguise as a precautionary measure." It's the kind of thing Mendez would have done if he'd been embarking on a mission. Take the precaution just in case. Start as you meant to continue. That didn't necessarily bode well for him and Kat.

"I know what you're thinking. I've thought it too. Is it a setup? Misha Turov plotting revenge for his father? It could be. Even though Yuri wouldn't likely work with the Turovs, he might not know they're involved. Assuming they are."

That was the problem right there. They didn't

know what the hell was going on or why this kid was suddenly on the move, visiting the places that made him seem like he was trying to find answers about his past.

The door opened and all Mendez's thoughts about conspiracies drained away as Dr. Butler entered the waiting room. She didn't look as relieved and happy as Mendez had thought she would. The hairs on his neck prickled.

"Is something wrong, doc?"

"First of all, the baby is fine. Healthy, and everything's as it should be with her." She frowned. "But Kat's bleeding a bit more than I'd like. Blood is normal and expected, of course, but this is a bit excessive. It can happen with precipitous births so it's nothing to panic over, but we'll need to monitor her closely over the next few hours."

A chill rolled over him. He'd learned the term *precipitous birth* just today. It meant that labor and delivery went much faster than usual and it could be dangerous, though complications were rare. "You can fix this, right?"

"I've given her something to control the bleeding. It should help the uterus contract again, which is where the issue stems from. The birth happened very, very fast, and that can cause hemorrhaging.

But she's here with us and we're trained for this. I expect her to recover just fine."

Mendez drew in a breath and tried to will his heartbeat to slow down. This was a situation report he didn't like, but he got bad sit-reps at work all the time. They dealt with the situation when it went sideways. Dr. Butler was dealing with this one. "Can I see her?"

"Of course. I've given her a sedative along with something for pain, so she may be groggy. But you're welcome to sit with her as long as you like. And you can see your baby, too."

His baby. A lump formed in his throat. He'd known for months, obviously, that he had a daughter coming. But seeing her for the first time, holding her, had shifted something deep within him that he hadn't known was there. He was a father. For the second time, actually, though he'd never been able to see or hold his son.

"All right. Thanks."

The lump grew bigger and Dr. Butler grew a bit wavy as she took her leave and walked to the door. Emotions swelled inside him, battering his heart and brain. He loved Kat with everything he had. Loved Elena, too. He would do anything to keep them safe. He would have done the same for Roman, if he'd known about him.

"You okay, John?"

"Yeah, fine," he said.

"Kat's tough as hell," Ian said softly. "She'll be okay."

"She's a fighter." Mendez swiped his sleeve across his eyes. He didn't cry. It wasn't what he did. "Thanks for everything you did to get us here, Ian."

"I'm glad you called me."

Mendez pulled in a breath. Let it out and pulled in another. Then he made a decision. He liked to think he used the same cool logic he always used when making mission decisions, but he knew deep down he was being controlled by an emotional need for answers. He'd lost Kat for twenty years. Lost his son. He wasn't losing her again, and he wasn't losing Elena. If there was even the remotest chance that Roman was still alive, then he wasn't going to squander the opportunity to find out the truth. He *needed* to know. If it was a revenge plot by his enemies, then he'd end it. But if it wasn't, my god, what a miracle that would be.

"I want you to bring Kazimir Rybakov to the US. I want you to do it as soon as you can."

Ian didn't seem surprised. He stood with hands in pockets and smiled. "You got it, *mon general*. With pleasure, I might add."

Mendez would have laughed if circumstances

were more normal. "You expected that, didn't you?"

"I've been waiting for it. I was pretty sure you'd change your mind eventually."

"Hell, I didn't know I was going to change my mind. What made you think so?"

"You hadn't held your newborn then. You have now. Changes one's perspective, don't you think?"

"If there's a chance he's my son, I want to know. I want Kat to know. Life is too damned short and too unpredictable to wait for answers."

"Couldn't agree more. If you will excuse me, I have an abduction to arrange…"

Chapter Fifteen

IT WAS DARK WHEN KAT WOKE. SHE WAS GROGGY and sore, and her breasts hurt like hell. She lay in bed and remembered everything that had happened since they'd come to the hospital several hours before. It had all been a whirlwind, but she remembered Dr. Butler and the nurses sounding a bit worried. She remembered holding Elena and trying to feed her, but they'd had troubles with latching on at the time.

A sound beside her made her turn her head. Johnny lay back in the recliner by her bed. In the dim light she could see his eyes were closed and he had a day's growth of beard on his face.

So handsome, her man. So protective and determined. He'd delivered their daughter like a pro and he'd talked her through the whole thing.

She'd been scared and in pain, but she'd put her faith in him taking care of everything, and he had.

She shifted, wincing, and his eyes opened. He sat up.

"Kat?" His voice was soft in case she was still asleep. She loved him so much.

"Yes, honey. I'm awake."

He sat up and took her hand in his, pressed a kiss to it. "How are you?"

"Sore. Tired. Where's Elena?"

"She's in the nursery right now. I've been to see her a few times."

"That's good. I want to see her, too."

"They can bring her in. Do you want me to get someone?"

"What time is it?"

"It's only about six. Still Christmas Day."

She felt like it'd been a whole day or more, but it hadn't. "Are you okay, Johnny?"

He pushed her hair from her cheek and tucked it behind her ear. "I'm fine, baby. More than fine. I love you. You scared me, Kat."

She tried to laugh but it hurt. "Well, I scared myself too. I feel fine though."

"Dr. Butler gave you meds to help stop the bleeding. Do you remember that?"

Kat frowned as she thought about it. "Yes, I

remember. That's one of the risks with giving birth so quickly."

"She says you're gonna be fine. The bleeding has already slowed."

"That's good. I think I'd like to see Elena now, please."

Kat knew that Elena should have been in a bassinet by her bed, but with her complications from the birth the baby had been in the nursery instead. Now she should be able to stay—and Kat couldn't wait for that all-important bonding time.

Johnny stood and smiled down at her so tenderly her heart ached. "Your wish is my command, Kat. Always."

Soon, a nurse brought Elena and helped Kat put her in the right position for nursing. It took a little bit of effort, and a lot of wincing on Kat's part, but the baby latched on and started to feed. Johnny stood by and watched, not saying much of anything. Kat looked at him from time to time, wanting him to feel like he was important to the process. He smiled at her and she smiled back, but she couldn't help noticing he seemed a bit preoccupied at times.

At first, she worried that he was still bothered by everything that'd happened during the ride to the hospital, but that wasn't really like him to dwell on something that was over, especially when it was safely behind them.

"Is something going on at work?" she asked.

He jerked the tiniest bit. It wasn't obvious, but she saw it. She didn't think anyone else would have.

"No, nothing at work. The world is fairly quiet. We're still on missions, but nothing outside the ordinary."

"You seem preoccupied."

He shook his head, grinning ruefully. "I'm navigating new territory here. I'm at a loss, Kat. That's all."

She studied him, not quite believing his explanation but unwilling to push for more. Maybe he really was overwhelmed with the new father experience. Especially considering how it had begun. "I know it's not the way we wanted it to happen. But we're going to be fine. Hopefully we can go home in a day or two."

He reached out and stroked a big finger over Elena's cheek, then hers. "I hope so too."

"You were amazing, Johnny. You got us through the worst of it. I'm so thankful you were there with me."

He frowned hard as if a new thought had just occurred to him. "Shit, what if you'd gone into labor like that when I was at work?"

She reached for his hand and squeezed. "Hey, I didn't. It's over and we're safe."

He squeezed back. "Are you hungry?"

They hadn't gotten Christmas dinner. All her plans to fix a turkey and trimmings had gone by the wayside. "Actually, yes."

"Want me to go and see what I can find in the hospital cafeteria?"

If Riverstone were an ordinary hospital with an ordinary cafeteria, she might be a little worried. But it wasn't. "Yes, please."

"Do you want me to go now, or wait until you're done feeding Elena?"

"Whatever you want, honey."

He leaned forward and rested his chin on his hands where they lay on the bedrail. "Then I think I'll go when she's done. I want to hold her again."

Kat smiled at her husband. She was sore and tired and more than a little stunned by the birth experience, but damn she loved her little family. "Merry Christmas, Johnny," she whispered.

"Merry Christmas, Kat."

Chapter Sixteen

MENDEZ SPENT the night at the hospital in the recliner by Kat's bed. They had a restless night with Elena wanting to feed every few hours and the nurses coming in to check vitals and monitor for jaundice, but by the time the next day rolled around and Dr. Butler came to check Kat out, she pronounced that Kat could go home later that afternoon or early evening so long as everything continued to look good. Apparently, the meds were doing the job and Kat's uterus was contracting as it should. They were twenty-four hours from Elena's birth, there had been no further complications, and

Kat was in better physical shape than most women half her age.

At Kat's urging he went home to make sure everything was ready for Elena's arrival. She would sleep in a bassinet beside their bed for the first couple of months or so, then move to her crib at some point. Mendez didn't know how old she had to be for that. He didn't know much about it at all. He'd read as much of the baby book that Kat had given him as he could, but he realized now that he'd missed a lot of it due to work. He needed to catch the hell up and get with the program, didn't he?

He showered and dressed in jeans and a navy henley, laced on hiking boots, and went into his home office to check email and to make sure everything at work was going well without him. Ghost answered on the first ring.

"Congratulations, General Daddy," Ghost said with a well of humor in his voice.

Mendez laughed. "Thanks, Ghost. How're things there?"

"We've had a couple of issues, but nothing requiring a general's input. All is proceeding as it should."

Mendez leaned back in his chair and tapped the keys with one hand. "I have faith in you. You know that."

He should after Ghost had run a secret HOT HQ in Matt Girard's basement a few months ago so they could assist Mendez in clearing his name and finding the real culprits who were plotting against the government. Without Ghost, he wouldn't be free and married to the love of his life.

"Yes, sir, I do."

"Need to update you on a situation of my own." He'd already decided that Ghost needed to know what was going on with Ian Black and Kazimir Rybakov. If Rybakov was an operative, they'd know it soon enough. But if he really was Roman, then Mendez hoped he'd be around more frequently.

"Wow," Ghost said when Mendez relayed the story. "How are you feeling about this?"

Mendez blinked. He hadn't expected that question, but maybe he should have. Ghost was perceptive. "Confused. Hopeful. A lot of things, really. If he's my son, then what? And if he isn't, what's going on and why the con?"

"If it's a con, the implications aren't good."

"Nope, they aren't. I'll deal with that once I know."

"I'm glad you told Ian to bring him in. Find out the truth once and for all."

"Not getting my hopes up, but if there's a chance it's him, maybe we can have a relationship with him. Or at least Kat can. He might not forgive me for the way the truth comes to light."

"One day at a time, Viper. That's all you can do."

Mendez shoved a hand through his hair. "You're right."

After a few more minutes of conversing about work and missions, the call ended and Mendez swiveled his chair to look out at the front yard covered in snow. It was so very beautiful, a white Christmas to remember. And remember he would, though not because of the snow. Elena Katharine, born on Christmas day in a truck not four miles away from home. He shook his head, though not without humor. He was finally starting to see the humor in it as the hours passed and mother and baby continued to do well.

He got up and went into the great room, folded up the blanket and put it on the back of the couch. Fluffed pillows the way Kat liked them done with a karate chop in the middle. He didn't get that but whatever. He positioned the battery-powered candles and made sure the timer was on so they'd be flickering when he brought Kat and Elena home. He put the Christmas music on and let it play softly, then went into the kitchen and checked the fridge.

The turkey was in there, still sitting in the pan and ready to go into the oven. Maybe he'd uncover it when they got home and take it out, let it sit while the oven preheated. Then he'd put it in and cook a damned turkey for his wife. If they got home too late, he'd fix it tomorrow. He wasn't unskilled in the kitchen, though he wasn't Kat's level either. Still, he could fix a meal. He would fix it so they could have their first Christmas meal as a family together. If he made lumpy gravy and his turkey was dry, they'd survive.

His phone rang. It was Matt Girard. "Richie," he said. "How's the family?"

"Hey, General. They're great, thanks. Congratulations on the birth of your daughter. How are you and Kat holding up?"

"We're doing all right. I'm at home but going back to the hospital soon to hopefully get Kat and Elena."

"Evie wanted me to let you know that she'd be happy to come and help Kat out if she needs it. We can also fix some meals for you."

Mendez's mouth watered. Evie Girard wasn't just a home cook. She was a trained chef and her meals were incredible. How Matt managed not to weigh six hundred pounds was a mystery.

"That's kind of you both. We may take you up on that."

"Sir, permission to speak freely."

"Of course. Say what you want to say so badly, kid."

Matt laughed. "You're a stubborn cuss of a military officer, sir. You run HOT with a tight fist on the reins, but you don't do everything yourself because you can't. Well, you can't do everything at home right now either. You have a newborn and trust me when I tell you this, you're about to wonder how anyone survives a new baby in the house. I've been on missions that weren't as difficult as soothing a crying baby in the middle of the night while wishing for just a few uninterrupted minutes of sleep. So when I tell you that Evie and I want to help you and Kat, you should really take us up on it."

Mendez couldn't help but grin. He loved his HOT family so much. They were there when you needed them and even if he was the daddy figure, the one who had to remain stern and in charge, he knew they had his back when he needed it. "All right, Richie. I hear you. I've got an entire Christmas dinner in the fridge that Kat never got to fix. Think you and Evie could do something about that?"

"We sure can. When would you like it done? Today? Tomorrow? You tell me when. We can pick it up and bring it home to prepare, or we'll do it there. Up to you."

"Can I get back with you on that? I need to see what Kat thinks."

"Absolutely, sir. We don't have any plans other than hanging out at home with our kids this week."

"I'll let you know. Thanks for offering. I can't tell you how much I appreciate it."

"It's our pleasure. Merry Christmas, sir."

"Merry Christmas. Tell Evie I'm grateful."

"I will."

The call ended and Mendez stood with his hand on the kitchen island, gazing around the space, and wondering how he got so lucky. His life had always been about work and duty, but this past year had added something that he couldn't ever live without again. Family, love, belonging. And not just with Kat and Elena, but with his team. Hell, even Ian Black was part of his life more than he'd ever thought possible. He wished his mother could be a part of it, but she never would be. His father was long gone. He'd been alone for so long, even when surrounded by friends, that he hadn't known how to let people in.

But he did now. He did and it felt fucking

fantastic. He took his keys from his pocket and twirled them while heading for the door to the garage. Time to go and spend time with his wife and baby. Time to enjoy every moment with his family.

116

Chapter Seventeen

December 27th

KAT WOKE up in her own bed that morning with her baby in the bassinet on one side and her husband lying beside her on the other. It had been almost seven in the evening last night, but Dr. Butler had let her come home. She lay with her eyes open, staring up at the ceiling and smiling so big it hurt. What a great life she had. Elena had wakened during the night, but not too frequently. Kat had pumped milk at Johnny's urging so he could feed her without disturbing Kat's sleep. She'd wakened every time Elena fussed, but at least twice she'd pretended to be asleep so Johnny could do the honors.

She loved watching him pick up the baby in his big hands, cooing and talking nonsense to her as he guided the bottle to her lips. It was such a beautiful, heart-warming sight. He'd said he was going to be an involved father, and he was trying so hard to do just that. Last night, he'd fixed dinner after they'd gotten home. It was soup from cans and grilled cheese sandwiches, but she loved it as much as if he'd prepared it all from scratch. Then he'd told her that Evie Girard was willing to come and cook their Christmas dinner for them. Kat, being no dummy, leapt on that idea.

Today, there would be turkey and trimmings and she couldn't wait. She'd talked to Evie on the phone last night and she was so grateful for all the help Evie offered to provide. Kat planned to do some of the cooking herself. Not too much, but a little, and Evie would do the big stuff. Kat insisted they had plenty and asked if Evie and Matt and the kids would join them. After some hesitation, Evie had accepted.

So now it was dinner for a small gathering and Kat couldn't be happier. Yes, she was still sore and, yes, she was tired, but she loved having people over for meals and the idea had her charged up. Since Evie and Matt had kids, they understood what it was like with a new baby. Kat didn't feel like she had to impress them. Which was good because she didn't think she could impress anyone right now.

By the time Evie was due to arrive, Kat was feeling more like herself. She'd been able to shower on her own, she'd fed and changed Elena, and she'd made coffee. Then she'd sat down while Johnny fixed breakfast. They'd had a good morning together and now it was time to start preparing the food.

"Don't overdo it, Kat," Johnny said, frowning as she moved around the kitchen. He had Elena in a sling across his chest and Kat's heart melted at the sight. He'd been a nervous wreck yesterday when they'd gotten home, but he was quickly adapting to taking care of a newborn.

"I won't. I'm going to sit at the island and peel potatoes. Mostly, I'm going to talk to Evie while she does everything."

The doorbell rang at precisely the moment Evie had said she would arrive. Johnny went to the door and let her in. Kat could hear her exclaiming over Elena. They came into the kitchen and she hurried over to give Kat a gentle hug. "You look fabulous," she exclaimed. "How are you?"

She was a pretty young woman with long black hair and violet eyes that sparkled. Her cheeks were red from the cold and she carried a basket with supplies that she'd set on the island.

"Sore," Kat said.

"Girl, I so understand. The twins didn't come anywhere near as fast as this little one, but I will never forget popping out two kids in a row."

Kat laughed. "I'm thankful twins weren't the case for me. Thank you so much for helping me cook today. Or cooking for me I should say since I won't be much help."

"Don't worry about it," Evie said with a sunny smile. "I got this. Cooking is my jam."

Evie got busy taking an inventory of everything, preheating the oven, and taking the turkey out so it could come up to room temperature before roasting. She made lists of supplies she wanted Matt to pick up before he came over and kept up a running chatter about everything she was doing. Kat was utterly entertained. Johnny came and sat with them, and when Elena was hungry he passed her over to Kat. Kat didn't even think twice about breastfeeding in front of Evie. She was comfortable with the other woman, though everything about this baby was new to her and it'd been years since she'd done any of this.

It'd been roughly two hours of talking and cooking with Evie when Johnny's cell phone rang.

He excused himself to take the call. Kat knew that meant it was probably work. She hoped he wouldn't have to miss dinner, but it was always possible. When he returned a few minutes later, she knew. He'd put on his poker face, so to speak. His expression was carefully neutral as he walked toward her.

"Do you have to go in?"

He nodded once. "Afraid so, baby. I shouldn't be long. It's a situation, but it'll resolve soon."

Kat frowned. "You can't know that, Johnny."

"I do this time. Promise." He looked over at Evie. "Thanks for coming today," he said to her. "I'll be back in time for dinner. Wild horses couldn't keep me away from an Evie Girard feast."

She laughed. "You've got time, General. At least four hours before it's ready."

He kissed Kat on the head and skimmed his fingers over his daughter's cheek. "I'll be back before you know it. Don't worry."

He hurried toward the garage, grabbing his jacket on the way, then slipped through the door. Kat looked at Evie. "I hope he's right but I'm not going to hold my breath."

Evie smiled. "I know what you mean. I guess if Matt's involved, I'll hear about it soon enough. Christina and Remy were taking the kids this afternoon, so I don't have to worry about them if he's called in too."

"It might be you and me eating all this food," Kat said with a sigh.

"We can call friends if so. I'm sure the HOT ladies would love to join us. Provided you felt up to it, of course."

Kat had never really had friends she could count on. She'd spent so many years alone, doing what she had to do to survive and keep her child alive. And then, after his death, she'd been on the run, in hiding, doing everything she could not to fall under her old handler's power again. Friends were not a part of that equation.

But now? She loved the idea that she had women she could count on to be there for her if she needed them. She was still getting used to it, but it was an amazing thing.

"I'd love to call some friends if the men don't show."

Chapter Eighteen

MENDEZ MADE THE TRIP TO BLACK DEFENSE International's headquarters, a nondescript building on a nondescript street. He'd been there before, but it'd been a while. Now he drove to what could potentially be a meeting with his grown son.

Jesus.

How would he explain it to Kat if this kid was really Roman? What if he was Roman but didn't want anything to do with his parents? Then what? Mendez's gut twisted into a cold knot. He hadn't considered that before, but it was entirely possible. Of course it was.

You'll deal with it when you have to.

He drove into the parking garage and left the truck, then took the elevator to the fourth floor. It wasn't Ian's Top-Secret floor, but he'd been there before too. The doors opened and Ian stood there waiting. Mendez wasn't even surprised. Of course Ian knew he'd arrived. He had cameras and motion sensors everywhere.

"Thanks for getting here so fast, John."

"Evie Girard is hanging out with Kat, so I was able to leave. But I can't be gone too long."

"I know." Ian cocked his head. "You ready for this?"

"I think so. What can you tell me?"

When Ian had called earlier to tell him they had Kazimir Rybakov in custody, he hadn't said much beyond that. He hadn't needed to. They both knew what the next step was and that was Mendez meeting the man and persuading him to take a DNA test. And if he couldn't be persuaded, he was still taking the test. Better if he did it of his own accord though.

"Not much. He won't talk. I've asked him if he's Roman Rostov. I've asked if Valentina Rostov is his mother. Nothing. He says he's Kazimir and that's that."

"Okay. How was he grabbed?"

"Returning to the apartment in Novosibirsk. He fought but my operatives overpowered him before anyone got hurt."

"Yet you didn't tell me you had him until now."

Ian shrugged. "You had other things going on. I called when you could do something other than wait."

"Fair enough." He'd have done the same thing if he'd been running the op.

They were walking down a corridor and Ian stopped in front of a door. "He's cuffed because it's standard procedure for an enemy combatant, which we don't know that he isn't yet. You ready for this?"

Mendez steeled his resolve. He'd gone this far, gotten the kid brought here. He couldn't stop now. "Yes."

"I'm going in with you just so you know. Non-negotiable."

Mendez gritted his teeth. It was yet another thing he'd have done too, so he couldn't argue the point. "Fine."

Ian pushed the door open and entered. Mendez stepped into the room behind him. Kazimir Rybakov sat at a table, his hands cuffed in front to him. Any operator worth their salt could still kill someone while cuffed like that, but Rybakov had to know he wouldn't get far if he did. He didn't move and Mendez let his gaze slide over a face that was at once familiar and foreign.

Kazimir looked up, his gaze sliding from Ian to

Mendez. That was the moment he blinked. Blinked again. He sat up straighter, frowning.

"Hello, Kazimir. I'm John Mendez."

"I…" He shook his head. "What is this? What are you trying to do to me?" He said that last to Ian.

"He isn't doing anything, Kazimir," Mendez said. "I brought you here. It's me who made this happen. Why did you visit the Yelchins' grave?"

His nostrils whitened. Mendez thought the kid was fighting some strong emotion, but he wasn't sure. Could all be part of the act and yet—yet this boy looked almost identical to how he had at that age.

"Who?" Kazimir asked off-handedly. "I don't know these people."

Mendez switched into Russian for the rest of the conversation. He didn't intend to beat around the bush. He was ripping the bandage off from the start. "Peter and Ludmilla Yelchin were raising a boy named Roman Rostov, who is supposedly buried in that grave under the name Roman Yelchin. Roman was my son. I didn't know him because I'd been told his mother died before I knew she was pregnant. But she didn't die. Her name was Valentina, and she meant everything to me."

Kazimir's eyes were wild, as if he were having

trouble processing this news. "If she meant every-thing to you, why did you leave her?"

"I didn't leave her. She died. That's what they told me." Mendez went over and took the seat opposite. He let his gaze slide over a face he knew. And the hair. Jesus, the kid had salt in his dark hair. He was twenty-one and he had a sprinkling of gray. A family trait. "I know you don't trust us. Why should you? But you look like you could be my son. I want to know the truth. Don't you?"

He didn't mention Kat yet, but he would. He sensed that would be too much at the moment. Once he got the kid to agree to the test, he'd tell him the rest of it. There was time. He hoped.

Kazimir swallowed. Then he nodded.

Mendez's heart thumped. "A cheek swab for you, one for me, and we'll know something soon. What do you say?"

"I know your name. I was forbidden to ever say it, but I know it. Yes, I will take this test."

Ian went to the door and a medical assistant was there in moments, taking cheek swabs from them both and putting them into tubes. Then the assistant was gone, and they were alone again.

"It'll take a couple of hours, John. My lab techs are good, but it still takes time."

"I understand. Maybe you could take those cuffs off Kazimir and we'll spend the time talking."

Ian tossed Mendez a key. "Your call, John. I'll be in my office."

Once Ian was gone, Mendez unlocked the cuffs and Kazimir shrugged out of them. They stared at each other across a chasm of possibilities.

"Tell me your story," Mendez said softly. "And I'll tell you mine."

Chapter Nineteen

Kat was getting worried. Johnny had been gone for nearly four hours and the food was approaching done. The turkey was almost ready to come out of the oven, though it would need to rest at least an hour before carving. The mashed potatoes were baking—yes, she baked her potatoes after mashing them with butter and cream cheese, thank you Pioneer Woman—the corn was nearly ready, and the green beans were next. They were also having rolls, gravy, sweet potatoes and a pumpkin pie. It was basically a Thanksgiving feast at Christmas, but that's what she'd wanted. It was her first Christmas as Johnny's wife and she'd wanted it to be special. Plus, she'd always adored an American Thanksgiving. She hadn't had that growing up in Russia.

She'd helped Evie set the table, and Matt had arrived to help finalize everything. Whatever Johnny's work issue was, it didn't involve Matt Girard and his squad. Evie was relieved that her husband wasn't heading off for a mission. Kat didn't blame her. That was one of the good things about Johnny being in charge of HOT—he didn't do missions anymore.

Kat fed Elena and put her in the bassinet she'd pulled into the great room. She'd managed to fix her hair and makeup and she didn't feel quite like death warmed over anymore. She looked down at her sleeping baby, then gazed at the twinkling Christmas lights and the fire burning in the fireplace. Outside the snow blanketed everything in white, but inside it was warm and pretty. Carols played softly in the background and the house was filled with love, laughter, and friendship.

"Thank you both for coming today," she said when Matt and Evie joined her. Evie was waiting for something to finish cooking and Matt was just doing as he was told.

"Thanks for inviting us," Matt said. "You didn't have to do that."

"I know, but I like having friends to share a meal with. I couldn't let you cook all this food and then not eat any of it."

"We would have been happy to do that, too," Evie said. "But we're also happy to share it with you."

"You should have brought the kids," Kat said. "It would have been fine."

"They are sooooo rambunctious right now," Evie replied. "I'm glad for the break quite honestly."

Matt grinned at his wife. "They're boys, honey."

"No, they're Girard boys. You were a very rambunctious kid," Evie said. "And Christina says you were hell on earth to her when you were both small."

He laughed. "Typical big brother shit. And don't forget, missy, that you sided with me over her when we started playing together as kids."

"I know," Evie sighed. "You were *such* a bad influence."

Kat loved the banter between them. They'd known each other a *very* long time. From friends to lovers and partners. It was so romantic. Like a Hallmark movie....

Matt cocked his head. "I think I hear the garage door."

"Oh thank God," Kat breathed. "I was worried he wouldn't make it back in time."

A few moments later, they could hear the door

opening. There were voices, as if Johnny was talking to someone, except he entered the room alone. He'd been on his phone, of course. Kat's heart swelled with love, like it always did, when she saw him. He smiled at her. He looked like he'd been through a wringer in a way, but he also looked happy.

"Hello, honey. Dinner is almost ready, so you didn't miss a thing," Kat told him as he headed her way.

He glanced at Matt and Evie, then focused on her again. He knelt in front of her seat and took her hands. "Baby, I have something to tell you. It's not going to be easy at first, but I promise it's an amazing thing. A damned miracle really."

Kat smiled. "A miracle, Johnny? What on earth could be more of a miracle than this little pumpkin right here?"

He grinned. It was almost as if he couldn't contain it. "She is a miracle. An amazing miracle. But I have another one for you. Trouble is, I'm afraid of how you're going to take it."

"Uh, maybe we'd better..." Matt said.

"No, please stay," Johnny replied. "Both of you. We could use some friends right now."

"Johnny, you're scaring me," Kat said. "Just spit it out."

He squeezed her hands. "Dmitri Leonov lied, Kat. Roman didn't die in that car accident. He didn't die at all. He's alive."

Kat stared. Her brain wouldn't process the words. And then it did and she burst into tears. Johnny wouldn't tell her such a thing if it wasn't true. No way. But how was it true? How did he know?

"I'm sorry," she said on a sob. "Sorry. I can't help it." She didn't know who she was apologizing to. Maybe her husband. Maybe their guests. Maybe herself.

Johnny wrapped his arms around her and squeezed. "It's okay, Kat. It's okay. He's alive. He's well. His name is Kazimir now. Kaz. Dmitri lied to you. He lied to Kaz. He told him you were the one who was dead, and they sent him into hiding with a new identity. Dmitri said there were assassins after you, and they would kill our son if they found him. He's spent the past several years in Vladivostok. He's a naval intelligence officer there."

Kat sucked back tears and forced herself to calm down. She had to listen, had to take it all in. Roman was alive. Alive and well and not dead at all. If Dmitri were still alive, she'd kill him with her bare hands. But he wasn't, and she couldn't get the time back anyway.

"Where is he? How did you find this out? When can we see him? Will he want to see us? Oh god, Johnny, I don't know if my heart can take this."

Johnny was vibrating with pent-up emotion. She could feel it in him. See it. His smile could hardly be contained. There were tears in his eyes.

Tears. In. His. Eyes.

Her big strong operator who never cried was crying. In front of people. She wasn't sure whether to be alarmed or amazed.

"It's a long story, but he's here, Kat. He's here and he's really our son. The DNA is unmistakable."

Kat blinked. "Here? In DC?"

"Here. He's waiting in the hallway. I didn't want to shock you."

She couldn't speak. Her entire body went cold and then hot. She couldn't move, couldn't process it all. But Johnny could. He stood and pulled her gently to her feet. Held her close as he turned them toward the hallway to the garage.

"Kazimir," he called out. "Come and see your mother."

Kat thought her heart would explode at the sight of the young man who walked into view. He was her Roman, just as she remembered him. Well, not quite as she remembered. He was a man now, not a boy. But he was still hers. Hers and Johnny's, so unmistakably. He looked so much like his father that it hurt. She could still see her little boy, though. Her sweet Roman who'd loved animals and wanted to be a vet.

"Roman…" She was speechless. Unable to move.

"Hello, Mother," he said—and Kat's limbs were moving again as she rushed to him. He caught her in his arms and folded them around her while she sobbed brokenly. So much time lost. So many empty days and nights, and yet he'd been alive the whole time. Thinking she was gone forever and that he was an orphan.

"I'm sorry, Roman. So sorry. I thought you were dead. They told me—" She couldn't say it again.

His grip on her tightened a moment. "I know. I thought you were dead too. I thought I was a target. Peter and Ludmilla died, and you were gone, and I was alone except for Uncle Dmitri. He took me to an orphanage and left me."

Uncle Dmitri. It chilled her to hear those words out of his mouth. "I'm sorry he did that to you. I would kill him if I could."

Roman laughed. "So would I. But he's dead and we don't have to."

She managed to push away and look up into his face. His eyes were glassy, but no tears had fallen.

135

He was so like his father. "We have much to talk about. You can stay for a while, yes?"

She wanted him to stay forever, but he was a man now and she couldn't simply keep him. He had a life somewhere, as strange as that seemed.

His gaze flickered up to meet Johnny's. Something passed between them, but she didn't know what it was. Understanding?

"Yes," he said softly. "I can stay."

Epilogue

CHRISTMAS DAY, ONE YEAR LATER...

"ELENA," Kat said. "Don't eat that. Put it down. No nasty wrapping paper in your mouth."

Roman—he'd gone back to being Roman with his parents, though he mostly went by Kaz with everyone else—sat on the couch and laughed at his baby sister as she looked at Kat with big blue eyes. Mendez watched his son, his heart so full it hurt. It hadn't been entirely simple, bringing Roman home and into their lives, but it was worth every moment.

He still remembered the instant when Ian had delivered the news that the DNA was a match. He'd known it already by then, after talking to Roman for a couple of hours and watching his reactions to the news his mother was alive. Still, to have it confirmed was both a relief and worrisome when he realized he was going to have to tell Kat.

His beautiful, strong, amazing wife who'd just given birth to their daughter and needed to recover. But no way could he keep it from her, so he'd taken Roman home with him. There were a lot of things Mendez still didn't know about his son, but maybe one day Roman would talk about his life after he'd been taken from the Yelchins' care. He'd hinted at it but hadn't said a lot. Not even to Kat.

They were a family now, though Roman had needed to return to Russia and his job in the navy. He'd been on personal leave last Christmas, which is when he'd decided to do some investigating of his own. He'd heard his father's name over the course of his job in intel and he'd determined to find out as much as he could about John Mendez. He'd learned everything he could through his job, but he'd wanted more. For that he'd needed to see the Tiger. He'd learned from Yuri that Mendez had been there with a woman who'd claimed to be his mother's twin. That had puzzled him because his mother had always said she was an orphan.

Mendez didn't know why Yuri hadn't told the truth about Kat, but maybe he'd decided that was a thing for Mendez to do when Roman finally made contact.

"What are you so serious about, Dad?" Roman asked.

Mendez smiled. It had taken months for Roman to call him Dad, but now he did it easily. "Just thinking about last year and how much has changed."

Kat's eyes sparkled. "It has, but in the best way possible."

"It's not every Christmas you get two miracles," Mendez said.

Kat reached for Roman's hand and squeezed it. "Every day since has been a miracle to me. I have my family. My beautiful daughter. My precious son. My handsome husband. You all make me so happy."

Roman kissed her on the forehead. "I'm lucky to have you all."

Kat sniffled. Mendez cleared his throat and studied the lights on the tree.

"I have news," Roman said.

They all looked at him. Even Elena, who only looking because he was talking and not because she really understood. She thrust a piece of wrapping paper at him and he took it, saying, "Thank you, baby sis."

"Well?" Kat demanded. "Tell us."

"My navy service is officially ended on January first. I will be free to move to the US, if I can get a visa."

"This is wonderful news," Kat exclaimed. "Why didn't you say so sooner?"

Roman's grin, so like Mendez's own, appeared. "Because I wanted to surprise you."

Roman had to return to Vladivostok and his duties last year, though he'd kept in touch over the past year. They'd seen him a few times and talked to him often. Roman had insisted he had to do things the right way, and though Kat had protested, Mendez backed his son up. It's what he would have done under the same circumstances. Kat hadn't liked it, but she'd finally agreed because she knew her son had enough of her husband in him not to back down on something he considered a point of honor.

"You will get a visa. Won't he, Johnny?"

Kat's tone and the look she shot him said that he'd damned well better. Mendez shook his head and laughed. "I'm not from ICE, Kat. What do you expect me to do?"

Kat made a sound. "You are General John Mendez and the president of the United States owes you his life. I think you can get a visa for our son."

"It's okay, Mother. I'll apply the usual way."

Mendez waved a hand. "I'm teasing your mother. Of course you'll get a visa."

"I'll have to find a job and a place to live," Roman said.

"You can live with us," Kat said.

Roman frowned. Mendez went to his rescue. "You can stay with us when you get here, but of course you'll want to find your own place."

No twenty-two-year-old young man wanted to live with his parents if he could help it. And not one like Roman, who'd effectively been on his own for years now. He was too independent, too much his own man. Mendez recognized it even if Kat did not. Probably because he'd met his son as a grown man and not as a child whereas Kat had a twelve-year-old boy fixed in her memories.

"Thanks, Dad. I'd like that."

Kat swooped Elena up before she could eat a string of Christmas lights. Good God, would he ever get used to having a baby around? Kids did the weirdest things sometimes.

"Fine, fine. I know when I am outnumbered," she said. "I'm going to get Elena and myself dressed, then it's time to start the cooking. Our company will be here around four."

Mendez stood. "I'll take care of Elena."

They were having a couple of friends over. The Girards couldn't come because they'd gone to Louisiana for a big Christmas at Reynier's Retreat, but Ian Black was coming, oddly enough. Ghost would be there too, and a couple of the younger officers who were far from family this season.

Mendez held his hands out and Elena came into his arms excitedly, chattering the whole time. "Dada! Dadadadadada!"

"Yes, baby, Daddy's going to get your clothes on. Mommy picked out your Christmas outfit, so we already know what we're wearing, don't we?"

They'd done Christmas presents first, but lunchtime was going to be Elena's birthday. When she was older, they would work harder to separate the day from the holiday, but for now she was a baby and didn't care.

"Want to come, Roman? We can talk about your move while we figure out how to fix hair bows on a toddler."

Roman pushed to his feet with a grin. "Sounds like valuable knowledge I may need someday."

Mendez kissed his daughter on the cheek while

she giggled. "Honestly, I didn't think it was knowledge I'd ever need—but here we are."

And he wouldn't change a thing.

———

IT WAS after eleven and Kat lay in bed beside Johnny, happiness pulsing like a drug in her veins. One year ago, today, she'd had Elena. She'd gotten her son back soon after and her life, which had already been pretty terrific, became even more fabulous. She didn't know what she'd done to deserve this kind of happiness, but she wasn't taking it for granted.

She turned on her side and placed a palm on Johnny's chest. They'd had a long day filled with family and friends and they were both tired. Elena was in her crib, finally asleep after being cranky about the whole thing, and Roman was in the guest room.

Johnny put his hand on hers. "It's going to be so nice having him around more often, isn't it?" she whispered.

"Yes. He's a fine young man."

"No thanks to Dmitri."

"Thanks to you, Kat."

"And to Peter and Ludmilla. They were good to

him, and they were honest people." She hesitated. "What will he do here, do you think?"

Johnny sighed. "He's been trained like us, Kat. Well, not exactly, but a lot like us. He'll go to work for Ian, probably."

Kat nibbled her lip. She didn't want her son in danger, and yet she knew what kind of man he was. She wasn't going to be able to stop him if he wanted to work for Ian. She wasn't going to be able to force him to be a teacher or anything like that. Nor was he suited for it, not with John Mendez for a father. She'd asked him about his old dream to be a veterinarian. He'd told her he still loved animals, but he'd decided his talents lay elsewhere. That wasn't going to stop him from having pets, though.

"Why Ian?"

"Because Ian can do what he wants. He's a mercenary. Roman will fit in with his group. You know I can't bring him into HOT."

"I know." Because Johnny was a military officer and the military had different rules. They were funded by the government, which meant they didn't bypass the rules they lived by in order to do what they wanted to do.

"He's not a US citizen yet. That will take time."

"I know that too." Kat sighed. "I worry about him, that's all."

"I know, honey." Johnny put his arm around her, and she snuggled into his side. "He's made it this far. He'll be fine. He's a grown man, Kat. We can't control him. Nor should we try."

She hated when he was right. "Fine, we won't try. But I'm his mother. I can fuss and worry."

He chuckled. "I think he likes it when you fuss. He hasn't had that for a long time."

They lay without speaking for few moments. "It was a good day, wasn't it?"

"A wonderful day."

She ran her hand down his torso, felt the intake of his breath. "You know what would make it an even more wonderful day than it already is?" she whispered.

"I think I have an idea," he said, pushing her back and taking control of the situation. She loved it when he took control. He was so fierce and commanding, and her body melted with anticipation.

He tugged her pajamas off, then bent to capture a nipple between his teeth while his fingers found their way to her slick heat. Kat moaned. "Johnny…"

He lifted his head. "I love you, Kat. I love our kids. I'm not the same man I was before you came back into my life."

"You're *my* man," she whispered.

"Only yours. Always yours."

"Show me."

He grinned, then lowered his head and licked his way around her nipple while she gasped. "I intend to, baby. Thoroughly."

"Stop talking and start acting."

He laughed. And then he took her breath away.

Afterword

Thank you so much for reading *A HOT Christmas Miracle!* I hope you enjoyed reading it as much as I enjoyed writing it. By now, you've seen the BIG reveal. I just knew that's what had to happen when I started writing about Kat and Mendez and a new baby at Christmas. What would it be like if they found out that one of the major defining events of their lives was actually *not* true? And by not being true, it changed *everything?*

I imagine you'll see Roman again. He's going to work for Ian, so you know he'll appear. And maybe one of these days he'll get *his* story. I know we didn't find out everything about him in this book, but that's because he has more to tell us, right?

Thanks for being a HOT fan. Your support means the world to me. I couldn't do this without you! Mwah!

Lynn

HOT Heroes for Hire: Mercenaries

Black's Bandits

Book 1: BLACK LIST - Jace & Maddy

Book 2: BLACK TIE - Brett & Tallie

Book 3: BLACK OUT - Colt & Angie

Book 4: BLACK KNIGHT ~ Coming Soon!

———

The Hostile Operations Team ® Books

Book 0: RECKLESS HEAT

Book 1: HOT PURSUIT - Matt & Evie

Book 2: HOT MESS - Sam & Georgie

Book 3: HOT PACKAGE - Billy & Olivia

Book 4: DANGEROUSLY HOT - Kev & Lucky ✓

Book 5: HOT SHOT - Jack & Gina ✓

Book 6: HOT REBEL - Nick & Victoria ✓

Book 7: HOT ICE - Garrett & Grace ✓

Book 8: HOT & BOTHERED - Ryan & Emily ✓

Book 9: HOT PROTECTOR - Chase & Sophie ✓

Book 10: HOT ADDICTION - Dex & Annabelle ✓

Book 11: HOT VALOR - Mendez & Kat ✓

Book 12: HOT ANGEL - Cade & Brooke ✓

Book 13: HOT SECRETS - Sky & Bliss ✓

Book 14: HOT JUSTICE - Wolf & Haylee ✓

Book 15: A HOT CHRISTMAS MIRACLE - Mendez ✓ & Kat

Book 16: HOT STORM - Mal ~ Coming Soon!

———

The HOT SEAL Team Books

Book 1: HOT SEAL - Dane & Ivy

Book 2: HOT SEAL Lover - Remy & Christina

Book 3: HOT SEAL Rescue - Cody & Miranda

Book 4: HOT SEAL BRIDE - Cash & Ella

Book 5: HOT SEAL REDEMPTION - Alex & Bailey

Book 6: HOT SEAL TARGET - Blade & Quinn

Book 7: HOT SEAL HERO - Ryan & Chloe

Book 8: HOT SEAL DEVOTION - Zach & Kayla

The HOT Novella in Liliana Hart's MacKenzie Family Series

HOT WITNESS - Jake & Eva

———

7 Brides for 7 Brothers

MAX (Book 5) - Max & Ellie

7 Brides for 7 Soldiers

WYATT (Book 4) - Max & Ellie

7 Brides for 7 Blackthornes

ROSS (Book 3) - Ross & Holly

Filthy Rich Billionaires

Book 1: FILTHY RICH REVENGE

Book 2: FILTHY RICH PRINCE ~ Coming Soon!

———

About the Author

Lynn Raye Harris is the *New York Times* and *USA Today* bestselling author of the HOSTILE OPERATIONS TEAM ® SERIES of military romances as well as twenty books for Harlequin Presents. A former finalist for the Romance Writers of America's Golden Heart Award and the National Readers Choice Award, Lynn lives in Alabama with her handsome former-military husband, two crazy cats, and one spoiled American Saddlebred horse. Lynn's books have been called "exceptional and emotional," "intense," and "sizzling." Lynn's books have sold over 4.5 million copies worldwide.

To connect with Lynn online:
www.LynnRayeHarris.com
Lynn@LynnRayeHarris.com

Made in the USA
Monee, IL
09 December 2020

51662861R00094